Afflicted II

Brandon Shire

Afflicted II
Brandon Shire
Copyright © 2012 Brandon Shire

This novel contains adult content and is intended for mature readers over the age of eighteen.

ISBN 13: 978-1480289857
ISBN 10: 148028985X

Special thanks go to

Blind LGBT Pride International

They helped keep things accurate and gave me information to dispel some of the myths surrounding blind people in general and gay blind people in particular.

Any mistakes are my own.

Author's Note:

This novel contains graphic depictions of unsafe sex. The author neither condones nor encourages this type of behavior.

You should always practice safe sex.

"We love the things we love for what they are."
— *Robert Frost*

Chapter 1

Horny is a funny smell and Hunter knew there was no purpose in trying to explain the buttery, coppery, unripe walnut fragrance to a sighted person. Sightlings were too distracted by visual cues to experience how the natural aphrodisiacs came off the human body and affected their partner.

Dillon had a uniquely horny aroma. Everyone's was different, but Dillon's was unlike any other. His fragrance held a trace of the exotic; a hint of the spicy Far East. It wasn't natural or unnatural, just distinct. Hunter thought it might be something in Dillon's diet or the cologne he wore which tickled his senses and drove him crazy. But he wasn't sure.

Hunter could smell it on him now as they lay in bed. It was a husky, raw odor which induced Hunter's lust even after they had just fucked. He inhaled and ran his hand across Dillon's chest as his head lay on Dillon's shoulder.

"I could be wrong," Hunter said, "but I'm assuming you didn't bring me all the way out here just for sex."

"Did you like it?"

"The sex or the cabin?" Hunter asked with a small grin.

"Both," Dillon answered.

"I always enjoy the sex, but the cabin is great too."

Dillon showed up on his doorstep yesterday and packed Hunter's clothes for a surprise trek into the mountains north of

Atlanta. First, he claimed he just wanted to whisk Hunter away as an added apology for abandoning him in the restaurant the week before. But the long, quiet drive to Helen had made it evident that there was much more on Dillon's mind than a weekend getaway. The further they drove, the more Dillon fidgeted and the more convinced Hunter became that the trip was going to be a last great date right before he got dumped.

He knew his anxiety didn't make a bit of sense. The week before they'd talked about Dillon quitting the escort business and how they wanted to build something more together. But he just couldn't shake the worry, no matter how unfounded it was.

He thought the reason for his apprehension lay in the fact that Dillon had dashed away for a week after that conversation. He'd claimed personal demands, but he never elaborated on what they were.

He and Dillon spoke by phone every day, and several times at night. Finally, it got to the point where Hunter thought Dillon was purposefully checking in to reassure him that he wasn't out with a client. That odd suspicion made the drive up even more worrying than he'd anticipated. Why would Dillon check in to assure him that he wasn't with a client?

The cabin wasn't very accommodating for a blind man, but Hunter loved it anyway. As soon as they stepped out of the car, he could hear the faint sound of water. Dry leaves crackled as they moved across the ground, and the forest chattered with noise as it got ready to settle in for the winter. There was no smog clogging his nose, no traffic blaring, nothing that interfered with the natural beauty of things and his ability to experience them.

Dillon described the diminishing lushness of the forest for him. There was a stream that ran over worn rocks and fell into a small lake, and warm wooden furniture that dotted the small, empty beach. The entire complex felt quiet and magical. Hunter knew he'd remember it for a long time to come, no matter what Dillon had to say.

The cabin's interior was scented with the residual smoke of the wood stove which sat empty in the center of the big main room. There was a small sink on the left with glasses and plates stacked on an open shelf. Frying pans hung from a few hooks on the wall. On the right, a love seat was cornered by two chairs and a small wooden table that left a path open to an enormous bed off to the side.

Dillon put their bags in a corner and watched Hunter do a walk-thru before he snatched him into an embrace. At the end of that embrace, their clothes were strewn around the floor and the heat from their bodies was warming the space between the sheets. Later in the night, when the chill really set in, Dillon climbed out of bed to start the wood stove. Hunter was snickering in the darkness as he listened to Dillon's grumbling.

"What are you laughing at?" Dillon asked.

"You."

"Me?"

Hunter chuckled again. "Yes, you. For a nature boy from Alabama, you sure as shit don't know the country."

"What do you mean?" Dillon asked with a small hint of humorous indignation. "It's not my fault they only have two pieces of wood in here. You'd think if they were going to rent out a cabin, they'd have some wood handy. Am I supposed to go cut down a tree or something?"

Hunter shook his head as he sat up further and leaned back against the headrest. "Cordwood is outside, Paul Bunyan. That's just kindling you've got there. If I had to guess, I'd say it's probably under the cabin."

There was a sudden silence. Dillon knew he was right.

"And how did you come to that conclusion?" Dillon asked.

"Because the approach to the front of the cabin is on a relatively flat piece of land, but I had to climb eight steps to get up on the porch," Hunter informed him. "That means they use the space underneath for storage."

"What about floods?" Dillon asked as he came back to the bed to get his shoes.

"Yeah, that regularly happens on mountaintops." Hunter laughed.

Dillon bent down to kiss him. "You're entirely too smart."

"No, you just rely on your vision too much, like most sighted people. You didn't see the wood under the cabin in the dark so you didn't think about it."

Dillon kissed him again. "See, smart. Be right back."

Hunter heard the door open and felt a blast of cold November air come in.

"Or," Dillon said before he went out into the rain, "I was so horny I couldn't think of anything but you."

Hunter smiled and slid down into the warmth of the sheets and waited for him to return.

When they awoke the next day, it was by stretching and wrapping around each other until their lust brought them fully awake and intertwined their bodies in a hard sexual foray. The sex left Hunter feeling slightly bruised and breathless as if Dillon was trying to prove himself. But afterward, as he lay with him, Hunter understood that Dillon had needed the bestial fuck to summon the courage to speak about what had occupied his thoughts during the drive up.

But even before Dillon spoke a single word, Hunter could hear the pain in his breath and reached out and tucked Dillon's hand under his cheek. He rubbed his face against it and squeezed gently, feeling Dillon's uncertainty at what he was about to say.

Please don't let him say he made a mistake, Hunter thought. He was worried Dillon had come to a decision that he'd voiced his commitment in the throws of passion and had since made a determination that he couldn't leave the escort business. Hunter didn't know how he'd handle such a statement.

"Do you remember when I left the restaurant last week? I told you I was going to see a client?" Dillon began.

"Yes."

"That was a lie. I didn't leave because of a trick. The call was from my phone service. It probably was a client, but I never checked it to find out." He retreated into himself for a moment and then let out a breath as if the ending to this conversation was inevitable. "Your mom…You know the guy she's dating?" he continued.

Hunter was instantly confused. "My mom?" The question threw him completely. "His name was Travis or something… I don't remember." He'd forgotten most of the conversation after Dillon left and really hadn't given the guy a second thought. He'd been too upset.

"Travis is my cousin," Dillon informed him. "My blind cousin."

"We don't have to talk about this," Hunter offered immediately. An instant sense of relief washed over him, but it was tempered with heartache. It didn't take a leap of science to understand that there were significant problems between Dillon and his family. Hunter had already been clued into the fact with the vague references and dropped sentences which occurred whenever they drifted into the conversation about Dillon's past.

But the odds that Lydia had met Travis at the same time he got involved with Dillon seemed…impossible. Yet it had happened, and the potential effect of it on their relationship could destroy him and Dillon before they even got started. He nodded to himself as he made his decision. He wasn't about to let that happen.

"No, we do need to talk about it," Dillon said as he reaffirmed his own thoughts. "There are things…"

"Why do you need to tell me this?" Hunter interrupted. "It's not going to change how I feel about you. We talked about that last week. Your past is what brought you to me. I don't need to know anything more."

Dillon squeezed him and kissed the top of his head. It made Hunter hope he understood how serious and truthful his words were. Dillon pulled his hand free from Hunter's grasp and ran it through his hair.

"I've done things I'm not proud of, Hunter... Shush," he added, putting his hand over Hunter's mouth as he started to protest again. "Please, hear me out. I need this. I need you to know. I don't want any of this coming between us. That's where I've been all week; sorting it out."

Hunter lifted his head from Dillon's chest and turned to him. "Okay. But so you know, it won't matter."

He could hear the rattle of insecurity in Dillon's chest. It was like a caged animal that had been trapped for too long, but Dillon wasn't sure how to unlock the gate and let it out. Hunter understood then that this conversation was about releasing old demons so they couldn't come back to haunt their relationship later. It had taken a week for Dillon to formulate the words and find the courage. Hunter squeezed him tightly in reassurance and lay back down on his chest.

Dillon began with Michael. He told Hunter how they'd had a little frottage and mutual masturbation and how he'd seen the sparkle in Michael's eyes when they parted. Then he went on to explain how Michael's kiss in the middle of the church had exploded into a ridiculous frenzy of condemnation which ended with him giving ten dollar blow jobs on the streets of Atlanta.

"I couldn't understand it," Dillon said as he shook his head, still in disbelief. "One week I was in school thinking about going fishing with my dad, and then the next I was wondering if the guy standing in front of me had a clean dick.

"I felt so...empty. I think the only thing that kept me warm was how much I had smoldering inside of me." He continued running his hand through Hunter's hair as he spoke, needing the comfort of Hunter's proximity.

"I spent my first night shivering under a tree in a park because I didn't know where to go or what to do. The money Travis gave me was almost gone." He shrugged still lost in his thoughts. "I used it for the bus ticket, but I still didn't really understand what my parents had done."

He pulled in a long breath and let it out again. Hunter quietly kissed his chest and ran his hand across it, cupping Dillon's shoulder as he inched their bodies closer together.

"I kept thinking about my dad," Dillon said. "He looked...hurt when he came back from burning the boat. All I could think about was how I caused that. But I felt betrayed too. That was our boat. We built it together. It was like he burned part of me and I couldn't understand why he couldn't accept me all of a sudden. It was like everything he ever said before was a lie."

He ran his hand down Hunter's arm and took hold of his hand again. He entwined their fingers and brought it up to his lips and slowly kissed Hunter's knuckles. It was a gesture of distraction, but it made Hunter realize how deeply wounded Dillon was, and how much he wanted Hunter's presence as he finally let it go.

"I can still see that first trick's face like it was yesterday," Dillon mumbled, his voice somewhere in the distant past. "He was so gentle. He just kept reassuring me. I honestly thought I could make it by pimping myself out." His chest filled again and he let it out slowly. "After I was on the street for a few months I understood more about how the game worked. I wasn't the prize I thought I was. Hell, I wasn't even a player." He snorted in self-derision. "I don't know what I was. Just meat, I guess."

He went on to tell Hunter about Shu-shu and his family and the animus he met there at the hands of Shu-shu's wife and son. He told him how Shu-shu had reached out. How he gave him hope with a few soft words, a bowl of soup, and a Chinese language book which he used to concentrate on when the life on the street became too much.

Then he talked about Roland, who had given him a break and taken him from whoring on the streets. He understood he was still a whore, but he was paid more. He earned a small space he could call home and despite how he usually felt, there had been periods when he enjoyed his work and the places he went and the people he met.

He explained it all to Hunter with a choke in his voice and then he breathed loudly and looked down at Hunter's face. "You look upset," he commented.

Hunter had no doubt Dillon saw the anger in his face. He'd felt it tightening his jaw as he listened to Dillon's story. But he couldn't stop it. He'd never been able to hide his emotions, and certainly not when it concerned someone he cared about.

Hunter reached up and traced his fingers over Dillon's lips. "I'm not mad at you," Hunter assured him. "I'm angry with your family."

Dillon slid his face into Hunter's palm. His gentle warmth and the stubble of his whiskers gave Hunter another raspy tinge of longing for the man.

Thunder suddenly exploded outside and they jumped in each other's arms, laughing at themselves before Dillon became serious again. "There were nights like this that I hated my family. I wanted them all dead," Dillon admitted. "But underneath that…"

"You still loved them." Hunter finished when Dillon went silent.

"Is that wrong?" Dillon asked.

Hunter shook his head and squeezed him tight. "No. Love is never wrong, even when it's directed at people who treat us like shit."

"Part of me thinks I should hate them," Dillon said. "And some part of me does, but it's still not as strong as how much I loved them before all this. It fucks me up sometimes and I get moody. I don't want you under the impression that you're the cause."

"Why would I think such a thing?" Hunter asked. Now that he knew the extent of the damage done to Dillon, he was ashamed of his own pathetic insecurities.

"Because I've spent a lot of time trying not to think about it," Dillon replied. "And I'm not too good at dealing with it sometimes."

They were quiet for a few minutes, each lost in their own thoughts. Dillon broke the silence first. "Now that you know everything, what do you think?"

"Honestly?" Hunter asked.

"Yes, honestly." His words were tense, languishing between anger and anxiety.

"I think the fact that you still love them is a testament to the quality of your character. I don't know if I could do that," Hunter answered truthfully. "It's easy to hate people for what they've done to you. It's a lot harder to love them in spite of it." Hunter chuckled trying to lighten the tone of the conversation a little. "I'm also wondering how I became so goddamned touchy-feely all of a sudden."

Dillon laughed. "You'd rather just stomp their ass, wouldn't you?"

"Just give me the word," Hunter bristled.

Dillon smiled. "My little ninja… I don't want you stomping anyone. And I don't know if it's a good idea for me to be at your mom's house for Thanksgiving. I assume Travis will be there. I don't want to make a scene at your mom's on my first visit."

"He'll probably be there," Hunter admitted. "She didn't say explicitly, but that was my impression."

Hunter paused for a moment and tried to frame his words correctly. "Listen, I don't want to seem like a dick, but I thought you said Travis helped you. Don't you want to see him again?"

Dillon opened his mouth and then closed it again, bringing

his thoughts together before he spoke. "I understand my parents because I understood how they felt about me. I was gay and they couldn't accept it. But Travis…" He shook his head. "We were tight when we were kids, really close. I probably should've told him I was gay, but I was a child too and I wasn't sure what his reaction would be. But…why didn't he come look for me after we were grown?" Dillon asked. "It wasn't like I was hiding."

"Did you want him to?" Hunter thought he knew what Dillon's answer would be because it seemed obvious. Travis had become the emotional link that would someday reconnect Dillon with his family. But without Travis' connection Dillon had nothing, there was no tie back to his family. And that blankness, that space which was Travis' absence from his life, had eventually been filled in with anger, hurt and a sense of betrayal.

"Yes and no," Dillon answered. "Yes, because I would've known he gave a shit, but no because he would've found out I was a prostitute."

Another silence grew between them and Dillon looked down and took note of the tight lines around Hunter's mouth. "What?"

Hunter shook his head. He didn't want to answer.

"What?" Dillon insisted, propping himself up on his elbow to look down at Hunter.

"I wonder if you're giving Travis enough credit," Hunter finally answered.

"Credit for what?"

He sounded perturbed and Hunter knew he had to tread

carefully. "Do you think Travis might've understood what would happen? Maybe not right at the moment you left, but as he grew up?"

"I don't get it," Dillon said with a growing hint of indignation in his voice. "You're implying he didn't come looking for me because he didn't want to hurt me?"

Hunter wobbled his head back and forth. He didn't think it was that simple. "It's just a possibility."

Dillon flopped down on his pillow. "You sound like you're defending them."

"No," Hunter answered firmly. "I've fought misconceptions my whole life, Dillon. But most of that has been dealing with my own misconceptions about the presumed motives of other people." He shrugged. "You've seen how defensive I can get. I'm trying to compare Travis' actions to the way I would compare something that was directed at me. People don't necessarily mean to piss me off. Sometimes they do something because they think they're acting for my benefit. That's all I'm saying. I'm just throwing it out there for you to consider. I'll still go stomp his ass if I need to."

Dillon was quiet for a moment before he chuckled and rolled back into him. "You would, huh?"

Hunter didn't know if the words had sunk in or not, but Dillon's sudden change in demeanor made Hunter think he'd consider the possibility. "Yes, I would. I can read the arrest report now. Two blind men fighting over a hot, gay stud-muffin. My mom would freak out and her gaggle of friends would make sure that everybody in town knew about her blind, gay son beating someone down over a man." He laughed.

"The scandal!" Dillon cackled and planted a kiss on Hunter's lips. "Silly."

"So, is that everything you wanted to say?" Hunter asked.

Dillon turned serious again. "Yeah, that's everything, and I appreciate the input. Now you know it all." He squeezed Hunter to him and held him for a moment. "I don't want secrets between us and I don't want my family problems coming between us either. Eventually, if Travis and your mom work out, and we work out, then Travis and I will end up meeting and…to be honest, I'm still not sure how I'll handle it." He faltered with uncertainty. "It's just… It's still complicated. But I wanted you to know where I'm coming from."

"Does that mean you're not going to Thanksgiving at my mom's?" Hunter asked.

"Can I think about it? I need a little time."

Hunter sat up, crawled across him and climbed up so that they were face to face, his legs straddling Dillon as he pressed his knees into the mattress. "Think about it all you want, but I still haven't changed my mind about you, and nothing you said has me worried. I don't know a single person who wouldn't be pissed off after experiencing what you went through. You have every right to be angry."

"You really want me to go to your mom's, don't you?" Dillon asked.

Hunter shook his head. "I don't give a shit if we go. I just want to spend the day with you."

"But your mom will be upset."

Hunter shrugged one shoulder. "It won't be the first time."

Dillon let out a long breath and Hunter felt his tension fade.

"Thanks," Dillon said.

"For what?"

"For listening, for being so fucking awesome. I've been worried about this conversation since we met."

"Since we met?" Hunter asked.

"Well, since that first time I came back to your apartment and groveled at your door like a freaking idiot."

Hunter smiled. "Hey, groveling is always good. But you had nothing to worry about." He leaned forward and met the softness of Dillon's lips. "Now I need you to do something for me." He rolled off of Dillon and lay by his side again.

"What? Anything. Just ask and it's yours."

"Ooh, I like the sound of that. But this is simple."

"What?" Dillon asked again.

"Can you open the window?" Hunter asked.

Dillon glanced at him. The request wasn't what he'd expected. "You want me to open the window? It's forty degrees outside and still raining."

"I want to hear it," Hunter said.

Dillon shrugged and got up. He pulled the window up just enough to let in the air, but not enough to get the floor soaked. "It's open," he told Hunter. He put another log in the wood stove and climbed back in bed.

"Listen to it," Hunter instructed. He cuddled up against Dillon as soon as he settled under the sheets and tuned into the soft pattern of the drops as he moved his hand across Dillon's skin. Dampness suddenly flooded the room from the chilling rain and sat moist against the heat of Dillon's body.

"We're listening to the rain?" Dillon asked.

He seemed perplexed and it made Hunter smile. Sightlings. He reached up, found Dillon's lips, and put his finger over them. "Shh, listen. Do you hear it?"

Dillon nodded.

"No, you don't," Hunter chuckled. "Do you remember the sex we had in the hallway when I told you to listen to my breath?"

Dillon nodded vigorously, his lips curling into a broad grin under Hunter's finger.

"Listen to the breath of the rain."

They were silent for a minute. Dillon closed his eyes and tried to grasp what Hunter experienced on a daily basis. Hunter moved closer and put the heat of his breath in Dillon's ear. "I want you to make love to me by the rhythm of the rain," he whispered.

They had fucked the night before, and then again this morning, but that had been hard lust. Now Hunter wanted passion and a slow, smooth rhythm. He wanted to feel the security of Dillon's embrace, the solid, unfettered motion of their lovemaking. And he wanted to make Dillon understand he no longer had to prove anything. He moved away and set his head on his own pillow, waiting for Dillon to find the rain's pulse.

Chapter 2

Dillon kept his eyes closed. A tiny smile lit his face as he focused on the gentle dribble of the rain. Small drops hit the panes and a distant rumble spoke of something larger and more dangerous to come. Desire welled in him. He felt the heat from Hunter's body juxtaposed against the chill of the incoming air and moved to it. He leaned into him for a kiss and ran his hands over Hunter's arms. Cupping the back of Hunter's head as he rose from the pillow, he tasted the soft flesh of his lips. It only tantalized the white heat growing in his groin.

His tongue darted out, a small, swift swipe to moisten his lips before he clamped his face to Hunter's. The thunder crashed again and he knew he'd found the storm's rhythm. Hunter's knees came up further, his legs spread, and the fire from his body called for the hard bolt now smoldering between Dillon's legs.

Dillon pulled a long slow breath when Hunter took his shaft in hand and brought the head to the center of his own hunger. He shifted his weight and nudged forward, stopping just before he entered Hunter. He pulled back and nudged forward again. Hunter started panting in anticipation. When he nudged his cockhead against Hunter's hole a third time, the breadth of it made Hunter's mouth yawn open. He pulled back and nipped at Hunter's earlobe.

"Do you want me?" he asked as he brought their foreheads together.

"Yes," Hunter pleaded, the syllables wet on his tongue. "Yes."

Hunter's need burned in Dillon, but he kept his movements in sync with the rhythm of the rain. The hot fluid from his cock gently lubed Hunter's ass with pre-cum as Hunter swiped it slowly up and down his own hole.

Dillon brushed his nose against Hunter's face and inhaled the soft sleep-musk he still had. He felt Hunter begin to pant and pulled away, kissing across Hunter's jawline and down into the crook of his neck as he slowly started to work his cock in.

A small gasp came when his head breached Hunter's ass. He inched his cock slowly into the tight heat. Hunter's legs came up and locked him into place. Dillon kissed his temple and sucked on his earlobe to gentle his growing lust. He'd take this slow. He'd worship Hunter's body with the storm as his persistent guide.

The rain came down in gusts, tapping furiously at the window until it slowed and began whimpering in little drops which splattered on the sill. Dillon matched his tempo to it, sinking in until he touched the spot within Hunter which made him cry out with a silent moan before he pulled back and slowly thrust in again.

All the fear he'd been carrying, all the worry over a rejection which Hunter merely pushed away with his arms, that was what Dillon moved with, that was the rhythm he used with the rain. He slipped into a quiet pace with the tempo of the winds outside. His motion was a slow metronome of liquid passion. He found it growing within him as he realized how much Hunter meant to him; how much Hunter's easy grin resonated every time he saw it, every time it lit his small world.

He turned his head slightly as he sought Hunter's lips. Hunter opened his mouth and he slipped his tongue inside and ran it along Hunter's teeth, teasing him as he rode him slowly.

Hunter latched onto his tongue and sucked on it, milking it as he would his cock. But Dillon held his tempo with the soft pattern of drops against the window and only allowed Hunter the tip of his tongue as he felt Hunter's ass clench around him and draw him in.

A fresh breeze ran across his back as the sheet slipped down and he moved deeper into Hunter. He wanted to push all the warmth and security he felt back at him; wanted to protect Hunter from the shivering cold with his own body. He'd not known sex like this before. He hadn't touched this level of passion with any client, only the motion. It still amazed him that Hunter taught him things about sex. Hunter showed him adjustments which turned sex into something more than just fucking. It wasn't the visual stuff, but the small twists which made a mastery of lovemaking: the smells, the tastes, and how his touches made Dillon understand the grasping need of another body. But Dillon also recognized that this inherent mastery came from the feelings he had for Hunter and not just from the sex, no matter its passion.

He pushed himself up, locked his elbows, and rocked his pelvis forward. His arms were on either side of Hunter's shoulders as he looked down. Now that he had the rain's rhythm he opened his eyes and saw the ecstasy on Hunter's face. Silence sat between them – silence and the gentle whimper of his lover's agony. He watched the subtle curve of Hunter's lust flash across his features and then observed the rise of his nipples as the cold air wafted between their bodies and made its way to the stove. He pushed in deeper. Hunter arched his back up as his mouth opened in a long moan.

He'd never leave this man if given the choice. He'd fight anyone who dared to suggest it and he'd face his family down when the time came. He would do it if it were the last thing he ever did.

As he looked down at Hunter, his heart filled and he finally understood what Shu-shu said. Loving someone gives you courage; being loved back gives you strength.

He felt the strength in his bones, in his soul. He wasn't the weak little boy he was when he left home, nor the insecure man he was on the trip up to this cabin. The clouds of that storm had passed and now he had only the rhythm of the rain between him and the man he was looking down upon. The man he was quickly falling in love with. But he pushed those thoughts from his head. Right now it was just the rain – the rain and the muscled body beneath him.

The wind was just a whisper outside, almost as if the storm had turned to snow already and dampened its own sound. Dillon moved even slower, allowing his cock to throb within Hunter instead of thrusting it in. Hunter's hands roamed over his back, a gentle caress that touched each muscle. His touch urged Dillon on, but not beyond the pace set by the storm.

In a moment the rain began growing in intensity, becoming a deluge banging against the window with the muted chaos of a maelstrom. Dillon matched it, his entire body vibrating with the power of the gusts that surge through him.

He stopped and gathered Hunter's hands, pinning them above his head as he positioned his cock again. He pushed into Hunter's ass and ground his hips down as the noise from his thrusts began to match the shouts of the thunder outside. Hunter whipped his head back and forth, lost in the turbulence of the whipping winds and Dillon's lovemaking.

Hunter tensed below him, gasping and begging for relief. He knew Hunter was about to cum and pressed his chest down to trap his hard cock between them. Dillon kissed him, forcing their lips together, pushing his hot breath into him.

"No, please," Hunter gasped. He couldn't handle it. He couldn't take the heat from their gyrating bodies rubbing against each another. "Oh my God!"

He exploded, his cum blasted between their chests and filled the small cavity in his neck as the tempest crashed outside. Dillon mashed his cock forward one last time. He held his balls to Hunter's ass and pushed, filling Hunter with his seed, the muscles in his body rigid with the explosion from his groin. He pulled back and slammed forward again as a second round of spurts racked his body and demanded release. Hunter bucked up against him, curling his body so Dillon could plunge in deeper.

"Yes," Hunter gasped. "Yes." He wanted each drop, each

small bead of liquid Dillon had to offer.

Dillon was panting when he finished; his body a knot of hard muscle and sweat. He looked down at Hunter and released his hands. Immediately they came up and wrapped around his torso, pulling Dillon down to Hunter's hungry mouth. He kissed him and felt the lingering juice of Hunter's orgasm mash between their chests.

"Mm, thank you," Hunter whispered when he released Dillon's lips and let him breath again.

Dillon slowly rolled to his side and Hunter curled into his shoulder again. Only after Hunter had drifted off to sleep did he realize that it was he who was lost in Hunter's touch. There was no other meaning to life when he and Hunter made love. It was just the two of them; just the want and desire which stretched out and went so far, far beyond the fervor of lust. He knew he needed this relationship to continue and he squeezed the sleeping man beside him; the man who had already acknowledged and accepted the fact.

Chapter 3

Hunter picked up his phone to call Lydia as soon as Dillon dropped him off at his apartment. He wanted Dillon at his mother's for Thanksgiving and wasn't going to allow Travis to ambush him. Cousin or not, if Travis made the slightest remark to Dillon, Hunter planned on mopping the floor with him.

"Can we talk?" Hunter asked as soon as Lydia picked up the phone.

"Of course," she answered with a hint of apprehension in her voice.

"Is Travis going to be at the house for Thanksgiving?"

"Yes, I thought I made myself clear," Lydia answered. "I want you two to meet. I assume you're bringing Dillon."

"I want to meet Travis before Thanksgiving," Hunter said.

She was quiet for a moment. "Why?" Her tone had changed from concern to suspicion.

Hunter winced. He should've waited before he called and allowed himself to cool off. But Travis had been the only thing on his mind since returning from the mountains. He could hear the hostility in his own voice and knew Lydia could too. "He and Dillon have a history. Travis is his cousin," Hunter informed her as he tried to temper his vocal irritation.

"And I'm assuming from the tone of this call that their history isn't pleasant."

"I…" Hunter sighed. "The mention of his name was enough to freak Dillon out the night he raced out of the restaurant. It wasn't a client he was leaving for. It was because you mentioned Travis. I really like this guy, Mom. I don't want to lose him over a turkey dinner or because of his asshole family members."

"Don't speak to me like that, Hunter."

"Sorry," Hunter apologized. Swearing in front of his mother in any context had always been forbidden.

"So if there's a problem you won't come home for Thanksgiving?" she asked. She made a noise in her throat which let him know how disappointed she was and how hard she was trying to hide it. But it couldn't be helped.

"Probably not," he answered. "I'll spend it with Dillon and we can go to a buffet or something. He hasn't said no yet. He's still thinking about it. But if he decides to go, I want to be sure there's not going to be a problem before we get there. I won't have him hurt."

"Why don't you explain what's going on?" Lydia said. "I've invited Garret and Toby and they'll be expecting you."

"You what?" Hunter asked, completely surprised by her announcement.

"I said…"

"I heard what you said. Why? After all this time…Why?" Hunter asked again.

"People change, Hunter. It…" Her voice became softer, filled with regret. She seemed rightfully embarrassed by all the years she'd berated Garret and Toby without reason. "It didn't seem right that they were alone. Working at the school has opened my eyes." He heard a shrug in her voice. "I thought it would be nice."

Hunter was silent. It was the first time his mother ever alluded to the fact she might have been wrong in her opinions about Toby and Garret. But he let it go. Dillon was his primary concern at the moment. They could come back to Garret and Toby later.

"His family threw him out when he was sixteen because he was gay," Hunter finally told her in a blurt. "Chucked him out into the street with no place to go. Travis was still a kid, but he and Dillon were pretty tight and Dillon is still understandably upset."

"I see," she said after a moment. "I'll talk to Travis and see if I can arrange something. Will Dillon be coming with you?" she asked.

"No, this is just between me and Travis. There's no sense in Dillon and I coming for Thanksgiving if there's going to be drama."

"I don't want trouble, Hunter."

"Mom, I…I don't want trouble either. Maybe you could ask your boyfriend what they did to Dillon. Maybe he can explain it somehow. I can't figure it out. Can you imagine doing that to me?" Hunter was angry again and he could feel it flushing his cheeks and creeping into his voice. He didn't want to tell his mother Dillon had been forced into prostitution to survive, but she wasn't a stupid woman. He'd already said too much. "Maybe we should just not come. Maybe it would be best," he added before she could answer.

"You really care about him," Lydia mused.

"Yes, I do."

"Do you think things will get any better if he keeps avoiding the issue? Maybe their meeting would be a good thing."

He shook his head, score one for the moms. She always knew how to make him feel like he was twelve again. "No, I don't think he should avoid it. But I do think he should face this on his terms and not on ours."

"And yet you want to confront Travis about what's between them without Dillon being present?"

"Yes. No. I…I want to make sure Dillon isn't going to be ambushed and made to feel worse than he does now."

She was quiet for a moment. Hunter knew she was weighing his determination and the fact that he'd likely come up and confront Travis even if she said no. They'd been down this road many times before as he grew into a man and cut her apron strings.

"Let me talk to Travis. There's probably much more to this than either of us knows."

"I'm tempted to say let's forget Thanksgiving for this year," Hunter grunted.

"No. Let me talk to Travis first. I won't have their family problems becoming ours."

"Okay," Hunter relented. "Call me back."

***

She called him later, just as he was about to climb into bed. "Well?"

"He'd like you to come and bring Dillon with you," Lydia

said.

"No. Dillon doesn't even know I called. He talks to me alone or no one until Dillon is ready for it."

She let out a long breath. "Come tomorrow night for dinner then."

"I'll see you tomorrow. Thanks, Mom."

He hung up the phone and began tossing and turning in bed. Did he just make the situation worse? Had calling been the right thing to do? Yes, he told himself.

But should he be going behind Dillon's back? He wasn't so sure. The mere fact he'd acknowledged Dillon's existence in his life now made Travis aware of the connection. Maybe you should've thought of that before you called, he chastised himself as he rolled on his side. Travis wouldn't have had a clue until Lydia told him. He wondered if he should call back and cancel. No, he decided. It was too late now. Travis already knew he and Dillon were together. He'd forced the issue even though Dillon had specifically told him he wasn't ready yet.

"Shit," he said aloud as he rolled to his other side. "Shit."

***

The ride to his mother's house seemed unusually long, even Bob was quiet during the trip and refrained from chattering with any of his inane comments. The stink was the same, but Hunter was pretty sure Bob's silence had more to do with his angry demeanor than it did with anything on the bus. He'd considered asking Margie if she could drive him, but at the last moment he'd decided against the idea.

There were already enough people tangled up in this mess and he didn't need to get anyone else involved. And besides, Margie would've wanted to know all the details before she brought him. That particular conversation wasn't going to happen just yet, though he had no doubt she'd get it out of him eventually.

Instead of getting off at Garrett's as he usually did, he went to the next stop which was closer to the center of his mother's small town. He caught the taxi he'd arranged before he left Atlanta.

But as soon as he opened the door to his mother's house he realized his mistake.

"Fuck," he whispered, hoping he could back out and bang on the door instead. He groaned inside as he heard the dying moans of passion and the hurried whispers of clothes and quiet voices coming from the living room. He quietly closed the door behind him and waited. What else was he going to do? They'd heard him come in, and the quiet stink of sex; a raw, sweaty odor of hetero lust, gave absolutely no doubt as to what they were doing.

"Hunter," his mother called out as she approached, flushed and embarrassed.

He could feel the redness on his cheeks, and for the first time in his life was thankful he didn't have to meet her eye. This was worse than when she walked in on him jerking off.

God! The thought wouldn't leave his head. His mom and this effing twenty-four-year-old dickhead having sex in the middle of the day like they were teenagers. And as she came closer he could smell their lust even more, which meant… Jesus…hot, sweaty sex. I should've fucking called, he cringed.

"Hi, Mom." It sounded as fake as her own greeting.

"You're a little early," she said with a slightly breathy voice. He listened to her adjust clothing and pat her hair down. He wanted to crawl under the door he just came in.

"Yeah, I didn't stop at Garrett's. I just took a taxi from the bus station. Sorry."

He heard her pull in a small breath of composure. "Well, come on in. Would you like something to drink?" she asked as she came over and nonchalantly led him into the kitchen. If she weren't his mother, he would've laughed at her actions. But he still had yet to meet Travis and now he'd have to do it covered in the odor of their lust. Could his life get any more awkward at this point?

He sat at the table in silence and listened while his mother filled him with chatter. Not only was she nervous about him meeting Travis, but she was covering her embarrassment. And then there was the fact that Travis was still in the living room getting dressed.

For a second, he wondered if Travis had a cock as big as Dillon's. But then he flushed with mortification when the realization hit him. It was his mother Travis was boning. I'll never show up without calling again, he promised himself.

He laughed inside. This was too ridiculous. Travis must be quite the man if he could get his mother to make as many changes as she had in the last two months. And he had her naked and moaning in the middle of this very Southern working day. Hunter didn't know if he wanted to shake the guy's hand or knock his head off.

His mother fell silent as the tapping of a cane coming down the hall alerted them to Travis' impending presence. Hunter listened as Travis came into the room and she walked to his side.

She directed him to the empty chair across from Hunter and introduced them. "Travis, this is my son, Hunter. Hunter, this is Travis."

"Nice to meet you," Travis said from across the table. Hunter thought he heard an abundance of pride in his voice; maybe too much pride. Had he planned on being in rut with his mother when Hunter came in? Was he that cocky? He'd gotten a woman more than twice his age in bed. Did that mean he was trying to show Hunter his misperceived dominance on their first meeting?

"Likewise," Hunter answered with an irritated tone. Whatever happened, he was going to attempt to keep it civil in his mother's presence. This was her home, after all. But if this asshole thought he'd be pushing him out the door, then he had another thing coming.

Lydia fluttered around them, refreshing Hunter's coffee then filling two more cups for her and Travis. When she finished, she sat at the end of the table like a referee. He didn't think she could miss the tension building between them.

Hunter went for the jugular. "My mother tells me you're not homophobic like the rest of your family."

"That would be difficult since she doesn't know them, but she's correct."

"Dillon is my boyfriend," Hunter said in a flat challenge.

"So Lydia said. How is he?" Travis asked.

Hunter listened to his proper pronunciation. It tried to hide the measured eagerness in his voice. He was sure Travis had heard it just as clearly as he did. Hunter was instantly wary. What kind of game was he playing? "He's doing well and I want to keep it that way," Hunter informed him.

Travis hesitated. "There are things Dillon needs to know," he said quietly. "He and I need to talk. We're not kids anymore."

"Obviously," Hunter replied. "But he's still angry."

"Does he know you're here?" Travis asked.

"No."

Travis was quiet again, considering his words. "Dillon's father is dead. He has a right to know."

Hunter heard Lydia pull in a small breath and Travis' voice turned to her. "Sorry, I was hoping Dillon would come for dinner or I would've told you. Maybe I shouldn't be here for Thanksgiving. There's just no way around what's going to happen. Dillon and I can meet after the holidays."

"What is going to happen?" Hunter asked with a protective edge to his voice.

"His mother wants to see him," Travis answered as he turned back to Hunter. "She wants him to come home."

Hunter felt a sharp pain blossom as panic seized his chest. *She wants to take him away from me.* "She's the one who threw him out," he barked.

"So you're going to decide for him?" Travis asked quietly.

Hunter was on his feet in a second. "Listen, you little asshole…"

"Hunter," Lydia interjected without adding anything more.

Hunter turned to her voice and sat back down. He heard Travis take in an angry breath of his own and Hunter unconsciously tensed his body. He was ready for anything the guy would throw at him. All he needed was an excuse. But Travis let his breath out in a calm, cool exhale before he spoke.

"I'm not here to argue with you," Travis said. "I don't want Dillon hurt either, but it wasn't me who chucked him into the street. I was a kid, just like him. You're taking your anger out on the wrong person. We've all been through hell, Hunter. And yes, I can only imagine what happened to Dillon. But you don't have a right to stand between him and his family."

"His family." Hunter fumed. If Lydia weren't sitting right beside him, he would've gone across the table. Travis was nothing more than a little, snot-nosed, fuck boy who thought he could tell him what rights he had because he was boning his mother.

"Hunter," Lydia said as she reached over and laid her hand across his forearm. "Travis is right. You can't protect him from this, and just think about how angry he'd be if he found out you tried to stop him from learning his father died. He has a right to know."

"I don't want to keep him from his family," Hunter snarled. "I just don't want him hurt by them anymore. Haven't they done enough?" He knew they were right, but it didn't make it any easier.

Dillon would be enraged if Hunter tried to keep it from him. He'd probably be angry about this meeting happening without his knowledge. But was it so bad that Hunter wanted to save him from more pain? Was that a bad thing? Fuck! He screamed in his head.

He turned back to Travis and put his hand on top of his mother's. He didn't want to end it like this, but she needed to realize that he wasn't about to take prisoners, not when it came to Dillon. He would fight for him if he had to. "Understand this," he told Travis. "If you, if any of you, hurt him, blindness will be the least of your worries."

He turned to Lydia. "I think I'll skip dinner tonight," he said as he stood up. "Can you call me a cab?"

She patted the top of his hand and went to the phone. Hunter went out to sit on the swing on the porch. It was still somewhat chilly, but his anger kept him warm.

Had he come home with the wrong attitude? He hadn't even given Travis a chance. He wanted to stomp him from the onset. This was supposed to be dinner and a few hours getting to know one another. Instead, it had turned into a few minutes with several threats thrown around. He cracked his knuckles absentmindedly. He was still so fucking mad about the whole situation that he could only guess how Dillon felt. He didn't have the love Dillon still carried for his family and he was sure he never would. Not after what Dillon told him. The only thing he could do was be there for Dillon and try not to fuck things up with his temper.

He ran his hand across the rough wood of the armrest on the

swing and recalled a time when he used to sit in this same spot and dream about having someone like Dillon in his life. He shook his head at his own stupidity. Meeting Travis by himself was a mistake. He should've brought Dillon with him, or at least given Dillon the opportunity to come. But that was BS too. Dillon already knew Travis was here. He could've called Travis if he'd wanted the meeting.

Idiot, Hunter barked at himself. Now he was stuck in the middle. If he'd just been honest with Dillon to begin with, he wouldn't be in this situation. Hadn't Dillon said he didn't want secrets between them? Wasn't that the point of the entire weekend they spent together?

"Fuck," he muttered as his mother opened the door and sat on the swing beside him.

"Do you remember when you were little and we'd swing out here at night when it was sweltering?" she asked.

He smiled. "Yeah."

His mind fluttered back and he remembered that he'd hated it most of the time. He'd often dreamt of the day he'd be able to get away. Back then, he couldn't wait to get out into the world and squeeze all the ripe juices it had. He'd wanted to travel and taste all the exotic things life had to offer – all the things people thought he should be wary of because he was blind. He'd planned on showing every last one of them that he wasn't going to be held back by their ridiculous concerns.

"I think I love him," he told Lydia suddenly.

She reached over and put her hand on his leg and squeezed. "When you fall in love you don't think of a reason, it just happens," Lydia answered with a small smile in her voice. "Your feelings for him aren't a bad thing, Hunter. But you're making the same mistake I did," she told him.

"I am?"

"You're trying to protect him from everything that happens when you step off the end of the porch."

He nodded and let out a frustrated breath. She was right, she was always right. "I'll talk to him. I'll tell him about his dad."

"Travis should do that," Lydia said.

"He should, but I'm going to anyway," Hunter informed her. "I'm not going to let this get dumped on his head. I put myself in the middle of it, so I'm going to see it through, regardless of what happens."

"Your dad would be proud of you, you know that?"

He turned to the sound of her voice. She hadn't mentioned him in years. He'd never known his father. Greg Stephens was a firefighter who died while trying to save someone in an apartment fire before Hunter was born. Lydia had always called him a hero, and, even though there were pictures in the house, Hunter had never seen them. All he had were Lydia's descriptions, a few faint odors from his old clothes, and a vague memory of two old people he recalled as his father's parents. But they were long gone. It had just been him and Lydia in the majority of his earliest memories.

"Would he? His blind, faggot son?" Hunter asked. He'd

always pictured his father as a big, macho guy not averse to making those unlike him feel a little less like people. But maybe it was the hero worship Lydia had tried to push on Hunter without realizing it made him feel less secure about what their relationship would've been like had his father lived.

He heard her gasp in shock at his words. "Your father never based his ideas of any man on what they were, but on who they were. That's what always counted for him. So yes, he'd be very proud of you, gay or not. Where did you get such an idea?"

He skipped over her question. "Do you like him?" Hunter asked as he nodded back toward the house. "Travis, I mean…"

"I enjoy his company. He won't ever replace your father but…" he heard the shrug in her voice. "It's nice to feel wanted again."

"Did I stop you from feeling wanted?" Hunter asked with a sudden twinge of adolescent guilt. Had all his tirades and demands for independence made her feel unwanted?

"Don't be silly," she chided with a tap on his forearm. "Even when you were a rebellious little brat I still knew."

Hunter smiled. "Moi, rebellious?"

She nudged him with her shoulder. "Got that from your father too. Probably for the best, though. I know I was a little overbearing at times."

"A little," Hunter chuckled.

She slapped his leg but said nothing. He realized it was the first time in years that they'd sat on the porch together and talked like they used to when he was young and still comfortable under her wing. After he'd left for Atlanta, it had always seemed like a burden coming home, and then he rushed to get away again. He had to get back to his real life which didn't include a coddling mom, smells of baked goods, or swinging on the front porch. Have to change that, he admonished himself. She was getting old and the news of Dillon's dad only emphasized the point.

The cab pulled up in front of the house with a tap on the horn and he hugged her and gave her a kiss on the forehead before he got up. "Give Travis my apologies for being such an ass. I'll try to make it up to him." Or not, he thought but refrained from saying.

"Don't worry about it. Call me when you get home so I don't worry."

He smiled and shook his head. She'd never change. In some ways, he'd always be ten.

Chapter 4

Hunter took a deep breath. "I need to talk to you about something important."

He'd called Dillon when he got back from his mother's house and asked him if he could come by the next day. Dillon probably would've come anyway, but Hunter wanted to be sure.

His problem was he didn't know how to start the conversation. He'd tossed and turned all night trying to figure out a way to break the bad news without hurting Dillon. But there was no easy way.

"What's the matter?" Dillon asked with a hint of concern.

They were sitting on the couch in Hunter's living room, two cold beers sitting on the coffee table. "Thanksgiving at my mom's house," Hunter began.

"Yeah, I know. She probably needs an answer, huh? I'm still not sure, but I've been thinking about it. I've been trying to figure out how I'm going to react. I don't want to make an ass of myself in front of your mom, and I don't want to ruin everyone's holiday either..."

"Dillon..." Hunter tried again.

Dillon reached over and squeezed Hunter's hand. "I'm still pissed and hurt and angry but... I'm also tired," Dillon confessed. "I realized on our drive back from the mountains that I want some peace. I'm sick of being angry and feeling like I have a hole in my life. I've got to face them eventually, I know that. And if you're with me…"

Hunter opened his mouth to say something then closed it again. "I went to my mom's house and talked to Travis," he blurted.

Dillon stopped his nervous rambling at once. "You already talked to him?"

Hunter couldn't tell if he was curious or angry. His voice was flat. Maybe it was disbelief. Perhaps he was thinking they'd just had a conversation about not having secrets.

"Yes, I'm sorry. I should've told you…" Hunter started again.

"Why?" Dillon interrupted. "Were you trying to protect me or something?"

His voice still had an odd tone; a crisp vacancy Hunter didn't like hearing. It made what he had to say that much harder. Hunter nodded slowly. "Yes."

"What did he say?"

Hunter was silent. This exact question had kept him up most of the night. But there was no other way than to tell him the raw truth. "He's going to tell you your dad passed away, Dillon. I'm sorry. He wanted to tell you himself, but I didn't want it dropped on you in the middle of Thanksgiving. I am so sorry."

Dillon went so still it was like Hunter was alone in the apartment again. He emitted no breath, no whisper of movement, nothing. He was just a blank space, an absence in the middle of the room. Hunter started to reach for him but froze his hand when Dillon spoke.

"Did he say when, or how?" Dillon asked. A twisted, squirmy panic had filled his voice. It was a desperation which spoke of something he'd lost and would never find again.

Hunter let out a shaky breath. "He said it happened a few years ago, but he didn't give me any details. I thought…I'm so sorry, Dillon."

"I need to go," Dillon murmured before he jumped up, grabbed his coat, and left without another word.

"Dillon," Hunter called as he grabbed the empty air. "Dillon!" he yelled again as he heard the front door close. He laid his head back against the back of the couch. "Fuck. Fuck!"

Chapter 5

It was still raining outside. The cold November drizzle seemed to intensify the moment Hunter stepped from the cab and made his way to the door of the Rat Hole. He didn't miss the fact that the weather almost perfectly matched how he felt on the inside, but he'd come here to get away from everything.

"Oh, so you finally decided you could make it," Margie said as he took off his coat and sat down. He was over an hour late and knew Connie had probably been riding Margie's ass since she'd arrived.

He felt her attention fall on him like a weight when he didn't respond with his typical banter. He wasn't in the mood for witty repartee today. He just wanted to focus on business. But he knew from past experience that she wasn't likely to let his melancholy go. Margie could be sharp and caustic at times, but her motives had always been well-intentioned.

Connie's heavy footsteps stopped beside the table and only then did he realize he'd missed her playful teasing when he came in. He leaned his cane against the side of the table and turned to her.

"The special?" she asked him without any of her customary sarcasm.

"That's fine. Thanks, Connie," he answered quietly. He wasn't hungry, but he knew he should eat. She walked away.

"Are you having a bad day?" Margie asked.

Hunter knew he had to tell her something. If he didn't, they wouldn't get a thing accomplished and he was frustrated enough. He needed the distraction of work. "Dillon's dad died."

"Oh man, that sucks," she said with genuine empathy. "Is he okay?"

"He died a few years ago."

"And nobody told him?"

Hunter nodded. "I told him last night."

"How did you know?" Margie asked.

"I met one of his fucking relatives at my mom's house," Hunter answered without going into the details.

"At your mom's house?" She was utterly confused.

"You know the guy my mom is dating, the big, mystery man I was worried about?" Hunter asked.

"Yeah."

He heard the slow nod in her voice as if she already knew this was developing into a drama. "It's Dillon's cousin – his blind, twenty-four-year-old cousin. That's who my mom is screwing. Small world, huh?"

"Twenty-four?" Margie asked.

He nodded when he heard her imminent humor. "I obviously forgot to tell you that part."

She burst out laughing and Hunter realized with everything else going on, they'd never had the chance to talk about Travis or his age. He'd been busy with Dillon and she'd been doing whatever she did in her free time.

Why don't I know what that is? He asked himself in a flash of self-admonishment. He and Margie had been friends for years and he hardly knew anything about her personal life.

His lips pinched together in a moue of frustration. This was the reason he focused on work so much. He hated feeling like this. It tainted everything he did and every thought he had. And it made him think too damned much.

"Your mom is a cougar. Go girl!" Margie hooted. She muted her chuckle when she saw the lack of humor on Hunter's face. She came back to the subject at hand. "How'd Dillon take the news?"

"Not well. He left without saying a word. He…He didn't just leave, he walked out. Like, out."

"As in out on you?" Margie asked cautiously.

He shook his head. "No, at least I don't think so. It just…He and his dad weren't talking so…" He fell silent. "I feel like I failed him," Hunter admitted.

"How could you have failed him? You didn't have anything to do with his dad dying."

"I know. I mean…I should've been able to protect him from it better, or something. Hell, I don't know what I'm saying." He stopped talking. He'd been replaying the moment in his head all night long. He hadn't found another way to handle the situation. Dillon's dad died and Dillon had to be told. There was no give in that.

She reached across the table and gripped his forearm. "Give

him some time to process it. He'll come back when he's ready. It's not something you can save him from. We all go through it eventually."

"Yeah," Hunter said. "Here I am the big fucking savior."

Connie came over and put a cup of coffee on the table. He felt her presence next to him, but she left without saying anything. Were his feelings that visible?

"Am I being selfish about this?" Hunter asked after he took a sip of the coffee.

"Selfish?" Margie asked.

"I thought he'd rush to me, not away from me. I just wanted to protect him."

"Don't be a dick," Margie said as she pulled her hand back in annoyance. "This isn't about you. Is that really why you told him? So you could be the hero whose arms he fell into? That's pretty fucking lame."

He pressed his lips together. Had he made this about himself? Was his reaction and the trek to his mother's house about him, and not about Dillon? He didn't think so. But perhaps Travis' proclamation about Dillon's mom wanting him back had changed everything for him and he didn't realize it. No. He knew where his focus was, even if he couldn't articulate it correctly.

"I just wanted to protect him. It just…hurt…a little." He stopped again, still unable to find his words. "You're right, it is about him. I'm a dick." He rubbed the back of his neck and twisted his head back and forth. He didn't want to argue with her. He hadn't slept worth a damn again last night and probably wouldn't until he heard from Dillon. It seemed like every choice he made lately was wrong no matter what he did.

"So where is Dillon now? Did he call?" Margie asked.

"No, he just left. I tried calling and left a few messages, but he hasn't returned any of my calls. I'm about ready to go over to his place and pound on the door until he answers."

"Give him time," Margie reiterated.

"People suck, you know?"

"Yeah, I do know," Margie answered. "So, why don't you tell me about your weekend in the mountains instead? I'll bet you guys had all kinds of hot, sweaty man-sex, didn't you?"

Hunter chuckled, a little twist of a smile at the corner of his lips. "You are such a fag hag. They should have a class just for you, call it Man Porn 101."

"Will it have pictures?" Margie asked.

Hunter laughed. "Let's get some work done. I really need to clear my head first. What have we got on the plate for this week?" he asked.

"Saxby is back, said he's got another one for us…" Margie began.

***

"So…about your weekend," Margie said with more than a hint of enthusiasm.

They'd gone through all their necessary business related conversation, eaten lunch, and now they were having coffee again.

Connie had been by several times, but she still hadn't said a word.

Hunter thought about how much he should tell Margie about the weekend and decided just to tell her everything. Well, almost everything. "Have you ever had sex next to a campfire?" he asked her.

Hunter heard her chair creak as she wiggled in her seat. She thought he was going to give her the juicy sex scenes.

"No, I can't say that I have," she admitted. "Not unless you count the back of a redneck's pickup with a load of cord wood."

Hunter smiled. "That's what the sex was like all weekend — hot, smoky, and burning." He sighed at the thought of the passion he and Dillon had anointed each other with. "I want to go back up there in the middle of winter when everything is covered in snow and it's dead quiet. So quiet you can hear your breath freeze in the air. I want to throw the windows open and fuck like Eskimos."

He heard her nod vigorously, from the bangles in her hair, and laughed inside. She realized it after a moment and voiced her agreement. "Yes."

"He made love to me in the rain, well not in it, but with the window open and…whew," he said as he blew out a long breath. He smiled, lost in the memory and passion of it.

His smile faded. "He also told me the reason he brought me up there." He thought about how much it had capped the weekend, despite their passion.

Her anticipation deflated. "Which was?" she asked.

"He wanted to talk about going to my mother's house for

Thanksgiving. Well, more than that, but it's what we came around to in the end."

"I don't understand," Margie said. "I'm not making the connection. Our conversation was supposed to be about hot sex, wasn't it?"

Hunter explained how Dillon had raced from the restaurant and how he'd almost called her when he got home but stopped because he didn't want to hear her admonish him about Dillon's job. An 'I told you so' right then would've killed him. He knew the client bit was a lie now, but he didn't know it then.

"He came back later," Hunter told her. "We had some really intense sex, and then he told me he quit the escort business." It was a short quick explanation which left out most of the anguish he'd felt at the time.

"But why did he bring you up to the mountains to tell you that?" He heard the confusion in her voice. He was telling her half-truths and she wasn't making the connections he wanted her to.

Fuck it. He was just going to tell her. She'd drag it out of him anyway. "Dillon's family threw him into the street when he was sixteen because he was gay. That's how he ended up becoming a prostitute. But don't you ever tell him I told you."

He paused. "Travis is his cousin. My mom wants us to come home for Thanksgiving. She also invited Travis, but that was before we knew about their connection. Now Dillon isn't sure how he is going to react to meeting his family again," he explained. "Got all that so far?"

"Yes," she said slowly.

He blew out a breath in frustration. "Dillon brought me to the cabin to tell me every shitty thing he had to do to survive after his family threw him out. He didn't want any of it, or his family, to come between us. He was worried about how I would react to what he went through."

He heard her glass clink as she tapped her nails against it in a slow rhythm. Now she understood the whole of it. "Can't say I blame him," she muttered. "What did you tell him?"

"I told him none of it mattered. I also asked him if he wanted to go somewhere else for Thanksgiving."

"Lydia couldn't have been too thrilled with that idea."

"No, that's why I suggested I meet Travis without Dillon. Of course, I wasn't expecting Travis to tell me Dillon's dad died either. I was hoping I could smooth things over and make everyone happy."

She didn't buy it, not entirely. He could tell by her silence that she was scrutinizing him again and trying to figure out what he hadn't said.

"You didn't go to your mom's just to meet Travis. You went there to confront him." She knew she was right and he heard the conviction in her voice. "You thought you were going to protect Dillon by threatening Travis and it backfired on you," Margie pointed out.

"I…Yeah, I did." He dropped his chin to his chest and reached for his cane. He started spinning it in his hands. That was precisely the reason he'd gone home. Travis was twenty-four and fucking his mom and he was a threat to Dillon. The guy was an ass-whooping waiting to happen.

"What else?" Margie demanded.

"Huh?" He lifted his head and put his cane aside.

"What else?" Margie asked again. "There's something you're not telling me."

He pursed his lips together as his brow folded down in irritation. "What are you, the fucking Gestapo?"

She remained silent, waiting for his answer.

"Dillon's mom wants him to come home," he admitted. Of everything he'd learned, this was what worried him most. The death of Dillon's father they could work through, that couldn't be changed. But his mother wanting him back was something else entirely.

"Ah, the crux of it," Margie said.

"Yeah," he said and instantly felt like shit again. It was what kept him up all night. He didn't want to lose Dillon, but he saw no way to protest or even be upset if Dillon decided he needed to go back home. Wouldn't Hunter do the same if the need arose? How could he go on a tirade against something like that? Yeah, the bitch tossed him into the street like trash, but she was still his mother.

"I didn't tell him about his mom, though," Hunter admitted.

"You didn't tell him? Why the fuck not?" Margie barked.

"Because I didn't get a chance, he raced out the door," Hunter snapped in reply.

"Did you plan on telling him?"

"Yes," he grunted. How could he not? "I wouldn't keep

something like that from him, Margie, no matter how much it hurt. I know I'm a self-centered prick, but I'm not that bad."

"So he doesn't know his mother wants him back, and you still have to tell him when he returns?"

He choked on his words and he felt her hand on his forearm again.

"Yes, which means I could lose him, and there wouldn't be a damned thing I could do." He blew out a long breath before he started crying. He'd never cried about another human being in his life, but the loss of Dillon might change that. How the hell did that ever happen?

He took a minute and composed himself. He needed to change the subject before he fell apart. "What's your sex life like these days?" he asked. "It has to be a lot less dramatic than mine is at the moment."

"I don't have a sex life," Margie answered as she withdrew her hand. "I have a dildo."

Hunter laughed. "We need to get you a man."

"Don't do me any favors. I like my life just the way it is, uncomplicated."

"Pfft." Hunter gave her a dismissive wave of his hand. "We could go on double dates," he offered.

"I don't think so. Seeing you and Dillon fawn all over each other while some leper is pawing me and trying to figure out if he's going to get lucky isn't my idea of fun."

Hunter smirked. "You have such a high regard for the male

species. Come on. It would be fun.

"No, thanks. Your drama is all the fun I need."

Hunter pursed his lips. "I'm going to ask Dillon to hook you up with someone."

"Definitely not."

"Why not?" Hunter persisted.

She was quiet for a moment. "What kind of man do I like?"

"You like hot studs like Dillon, I guess."

She grunted at him, showing his obvious ignorance. "A woman like me wouldn't have a chance with someone like Dillon. The fantasy is great, but most of the straight men that look like him are too wrapped up in themselves, and they damned sure aren't looking for someone of my body type."

"Please. You don't give yourself credit."

"Hunter, you know what? I've been fat my whole life. I've accepted that. I really don't give a shit what anyone thinks. I have no plans to be anyone's mercy fuck and that's all I'd be getting from someone like Dillon. So please, I appreciate the idea, but I got this. Besides…"

Hunter heard the change in her inflection and knew she hadn't meant to add anything further. He was going to argue he'd had the very same thoughts about Dillon at first, but he honed in on what she wasn't saying, just like she'd done to him. "Besides what?" he asked.

"Nothing," she answered.

"Oh no, you're not getting off that easy," Hunter argued.

"Speak. You've dragged me over the coals enough today."

He thought about how they'd first met and how she'd come in for an interview and quickly made it known she didn't care that he was blind or gay. She'd wanted to work with someone who was professional, had a solid business plan, and had the drive to succeed. He loved her candor, but in the years that followed, he noticed how rarely she mentioned her actual love life. They often talked about some of the men she'd had sex with, most of whom she thought were losers, but he could only recall a handful of conversations which went beyond the sexual aspect.

"I'm an insensitive, self-centered, douchebag who hasn't paid attention to my bestie since we've known each other. Isn't that the sustenance of everything you just said?" Hunter asked. "Well, now I'm asking. Now I'm paying attention. Besides what?"

"And how did I say all that?" she asked.

"By asking me what type of men you like and throwing the guilt back on me for being such a self-centered fag. Your implication is that I've never even bothered to ask what your life is like or what type of man you wanted to make it complete."

She laughed at him. "And I'm just supposed to spit it out for you?"

"Yes," Hunter answered. "For all the past sins I have committed against you, I'm asking. I'd like to help. I'd like you to feel as happy as I do when I'm with Dillon."

"I'm bisexual, Hunter. Or at least I've been considering it," she offered, her voice tapering off to almost a whisper.

"What? Since when?"

"See what I mean? You think you know me, but you don't."

He was shocked into silence. What the fuck was up with all the women in his life lately? "But you never said anything, how would I know? You've only talked about men."

"No, you've only talked about men," Margie replied. "Or work, or your mom, or…whatever."

"We'll get you a lesbian then," Hunter announced.

"No, you won't. How many lesbians do you know anyway? You think you can just buy one at the farmer's market?"

"I could find one or two. This is Atlanta for Christ's sake."

"No, thanks. I already have one."

His mouth hung open. "No fucking way." He hadn't meant it to come out like sheer disbelief, but it did. He recovered quickly, hoping she didn't think he considered the idea impossible. If anyone, he'd like to see her happy too. "You've been holding out big time. Give me the details, woman."

He heard her snicker with something just a bit more than humor. "It just sort of happened this past week, it's nothing yet. It's not like you and Dillon. We're just hanging out, kind of feeling each other out."

"Have you fucked her yet?"

"Hunter!"

"Please, don't go all high and mighty on me now. How often have you asked me that question?" Hunter reminded her.

"We've…messed around."

"Uh," he blew his breath out at her. "I can see this line of conversation is going nowhere. What's she like? You can at least tell me that."

"She's the jealous type. And that's why I'm not sure," Margie admitted.

Hunter was quiet for a moment, tapping his lips with his index finger. "But it's nice, isn't it? Having someone jealous about you?"

"I guess, but I can also see it leading to problems down the road. I don't need another psycho in my life."

Another? Hunter asked himself. When was the first one? "So she's jealous, what else?"

"She's black."

He was expecting more, but he realized Margie was waiting for his reaction to the news. "What the fuck does that have to do with it? If she makes you happy, fuck what other people think."

"Yeah well, she's got a big family and she's this tiny, fierce, little black woman and I'm a big, fat white girl. I'm not sure what to expect."

Her statement caught Hunter off guard. Was that really how she saw herself? It made no sense to him. He'd never had anything but admiration for Margie. She was one of the most beautiful people he knew. She could be abrasive, just like him, but inside she was all heart.

"What does she say?" he asked as he felt his conscience cramp with the comment he made to Dillon about having fatties in his bed. She probably knew more about discrimination than he did. Most people felt sorry for him. He didn't want their fucking pity, but he doubted that was how they'd view her. It just re-emphasized to him how much people sucked.

"She doesn't give a fuck what anyone says. Her brothers are all six-foot-four, two-hundred-eighty pounds and they're terrified of her." She laughed. "She said they were the first boys she beat up as a kid. The only girl in a house full of six kids," she added.

"So when do we meet?"

"Not for a while yet, if ever. I'm not in any hurry. As I said, this isn't you and Dillon."

"What about your family?" Hunter threw out. He'd prattled on constantly about his mom since they had known each other, and now he was talking about Dillon's family. Yet, in all that time, Margie had never mentioned her own family except in the vaguest regard. She'd spoken of her brother and the animus with her parents, but nothing more. He could hear her rubbing and probing her arm. She'd said she'd broken it as a child but never mentioned how. He thought there was more to the story, but never asked.

She seemed to stumble over the question. He wondered if it was in surprise. He couldn't recall ever having asked about her family so directly.

"Irrelevant," she answered.

He nodded. There was something behind her reticence and he had to ask himself why it had taken him so long to notice. Maybe he really was self-centered. "I'm going to the dojo for a few hours," he said as he checked his watch. "I need to work out some of this stress." He was giving her an out and they both knew it.

"I don't know if you go to the dojo to have a workout, or because you like the man smell so much," Margie quipped.

"Don't be jealous. If things don't work out between you and…What's her name?" Hunter asked.

"Lilly."

"Yeah, well, if things don't work out between you and Lilly, I might bring a jockstrap home for you. Just think of all that sweaty man smell."

"You are so fucking gross."

He stood and made a show of holding a jockstrap up to his nose as he inhaled deeply. "Man smells. Love them!"

They laughed together.

"Thanks, Margie."

"Sure, let me know what happens with Dillon."

He scoffed. "As if I could keep it from you anyway. I think you're worse than my mom sometimes."

"I could be on her payroll."

He smiled. "I wouldn't doubt it."

"For the record," she said. "Fight for him if you have to, but let him deal with the battles with his family. You'll lose there every time."

"You like him," Hunter mused. "I didn't think you did."

"I like what he's doing to you," Margie replied.

"Which is?"

"Making you less of an asshole," she said and started laughing.

He smiled. He had to admit she was right.

Chapter 6

It was very late when the downstairs buzzer rang. Hunter knew none of his neighbors would be pressing the damned thing at this hour and he jumped out of bed with the sure knowledge that it could only be Dillon.

"Yes?" he asked when he keyed the microphone.

"It's me," Dillon answered.

His voice sounded weary and defeated. Hunter opened the door and waited, listening to his heavy footsteps as he came up the stairs. Hunter could tell right away that he was unwashed and probably looked as unkempt as he smelled. It wasn't the usual luscious odor which hung around him but one of stale melancholy, a lost despondency which had likely wandered with him over the last three days of his absence.

He slipped his arms around Hunter without a word and pulled him close. Hunter shut the door and wrapped his own arms equality tight around him. Dillon bent his neck to Hunter's shoulder and began to sob. His cries became a weight; a mass that was more than either of them could tolerate. His body went limp with his tears, dragging them to the floor as Hunter pulled Dillon tight to his chest to keep them from falling over.

Hunter turned them and sat with his back against the wall and let Dillon curl into his lap, stroking his hair as the grief took a hold of Dillon's body and racked it with shudders.

Hunter cooed to him like a small child, reassuring him with his touch. He could not take this pain from him and he shed his own tears with Dillon because of it.

He sat for an hour listening to Dillon's sorrow before the tears began to taper off and the heaves began to slow. Hunter continued stroking his lank hair and felt a small peace come over Dillon as the fatigue took hold and he drifted off into an exhausted sleep in Hunter's lap.

"I'm so sorry, baby," he whispered as he bent and kissed the side of Dillon's head. "So, so sorry."

Hunter woke several hours later from the pain in his legs and pressure of Dillon's weight still curled up on them. He could feel the apartment warming and knew the sun must be up. He began to move and slide from under Dillon until his voice stopped all movement.

"Do you think he hated me when he died?" Dillon asked quietly.

The pain in his legs was forgotten at once. "No. I think he probably regretted what happened. Most people don't go to their grave with hate, Dillon. They look back and see all the things they could've done better. That's why repentance has always been such a big part of the dying process for people, especially for Christians. We do stupid things which we later regret but don't know how to undo. I think, if anything, that's where your dad was when he passed."

Dillon pushed himself up and sat against the wall beside Hunter so their shoulders were touching. "I went to see his grave.

I…I had to go. I'm sorry I ran out of here like I did."

Hunter reached over, found his face and turned it to him. He didn't kiss Dillon. He just ran his thumb across the soft, warm surface of Dillon's lips. He'd been terrified he'd never feel their touch again. "You don't have anything to be sorry about."

Dillon pulled a long, deep breath. "It's not how I wanted things to end between me and my dad. I thought things would be different. I thought I'd have a chance to explain…that we'd have time…"

Hunter was quiet beside him, letting the words come out as he knew they must. Dillon had shed the tears, but it would be a long while before he'd shed the pain he'd harbored for so long.

"I went and saw Travis too," Dillon said after a minute of silent contemplation.

"How'd you find him?"

"Your mom said he worked at the blind school, remember? It wasn't hard. I just caught him at work. We didn't get a chance to talk much. He wanted me to come back later, but I never did."

He was quiet for a moment and Hunter reached over until he found his hand. He gave it a squeeze as Dillon spoke again.

"He said my mom wants to see me. She wants me to come home. Did he tell you that?" Dillon asked.

The tone of his question wasn't damning, but it could change in an instant and Hunter knew it. "Yes." He winced and waited for Dillon's harsh reaction. "I wanted to tell you, but you left so fast," he added quickly.

"I don't think I'm going to," Dillon continued, the bleakness of his voice telling Hunter his thoughts were focused internally and not on Hunter's words. "She was the one who drove me out. All that religious shit…It was her. We wouldn't even have been in the goddamned church if it weren't for her."

Hunter listened quietly. He stretched his legs to let the blood flow back into them before he tried to stand.

"I parked in front of the house for hours just looking at it," Dillon muttered. "I kept thinking about all the things me and my dad used to do together." His voice was bruised. "Travis said she was the only one there when he died. I don't know if I can ever forgive her." He paused and looked at Hunter. "Could you? Do you think he wanted me there? In the end, I mean?"

Hunter considered his questions, they sounded like small hopes which would ease his pain and then tinge his despair with further regret. "I don't know how I'd react. I don't think it's a question anyone except you can answer. As for your dad wanting you there…I'm sure of it."

Dillon let out a long breath. "I need to take a shower. I smell disgusting and here I am rubbing all over you."

"Don't worry about it." He kissed the side of Dillon's cheek. It tasted like tears and sweat. If he weren't positive that Dillon still needed some time alone, Hunter would've put him in the tub and washed him while he soaked. "Go take a shower." He nodded towards the bathroom. "I'll make breakfast. When was the last time you ate?"

"I'm not sure, a couple of days ago maybe. I haven't been hungry."

Hunter nudged him with his shoulder. "Go on. I'll whip something up."

"You have anything I can wear?" he asked as he rose to his feet. "These clothes need to be washed."

"Just take what you need out of my bedroom. You should fit into something."

Hunter could still smell the salt of his tears on his hands and face when Dillon squatted in front of him and gave him a soft kiss. "Thanks," he said before he stood up and went to the bathroom.

Hunter nodded. "Sure." What else could he say? His emotions were still just as raw and numb as Dillon's had been. But all he could articulate inside his head was the realization that they'd survived. Dillon wasn't mad at him and now he didn't have to break the news about his mother.

Was that selfish? he questioned himself with a sharp pang of guilt. It was a relief that he didn't have to initiate the conversation but was it selfish to be pleased by the fact? He'd just wanted them to survive. If it took selfishness, well, he was going to be goddamned selfish. He had to. Dillon already owned more of his heart than he thought anyone ever could, and he didn't know if he could give him up.

He got up off the floor and picked up the phone as Dillon went into the bathroom. He dialed once he heard the water start and the shower door click shut.

"What's up?" Margie asked from the other end of the line.

"I'm not going to be in today; maybe not tomorrow either. If we have any appointments or studio time, then reschedule them," Hunter instructed her.

"Is he back?" Margie asked, lowering her voice to a whisper.

"Yeah."

"How is he?"

"As you'd expect. He's in the shower. I'm going to make breakfast and we're going to chill today if he wants to. If not, I'll call you back."

"Should I wait before I cancel anything?" she asked. "We have the studio booked for a session and the kid coming in from Augusta for the new book tomorrow."

Hunter thought for a moment. He wouldn't have been able to function today even if Dillon hadn't come back. He was just too damned tired from lack of sleep. "Go ahead and cancel both. Call the kid and tell him it's a family emergency or something. If he can't understand, tough shit, we'll find someone else. The studio…" He ran his hand through his hair as he considered it. They'd charge him whether he showed up or not. "Fuck the studio. I'll just pay for the session out of personal funds."

"One more thing," Margie said.

"What?"

"Take him out to eat, don't make him suffer through your cooking." She hung up before he could respond.

He smirked when he heard the click of her disconnect. But

her jibe got him thinking about something his mother had said many years ago. "You might be right," he mused as he put the phone down and went to the kitchen.

He got the coffee going and quickly realized that he needed to take a long, hard piss. This wasn't about to wait. The door to the bathroom was still open so he announced his presence and went to relieve himself, sighing in front of the bowl as he let go.

He heard Dillon chuckle from the shower behind him. "I felt exactly the same way."

"Thought I was going to burst."

"Want to join me?" Dillon asked.

Hunter considered it for a moment. He wanted to get a little food into Dillon and pull his mental state up a few notches. Sex might help, but it might it also remind him of why he was estranged from his father in the first place. "No, you go ahead. I've got breakfast going. I'll take one after we eat."

"You don't know what you're missing," Dillon called playfully.

"Yeah, I do," Hunter murmured as he went back to the kitchen. He could still hear the melancholy in Dillon's voice, and even though he thought they'd both enjoy sex despite how tired they were, Dillon needed food and some serious rest before anything else.

***

The coffee was hot, the toast was cold, and the bacon was burnt to a crisp when Dillon came into the kitchen. Hunter heard

Dillon's bare feet on the floor and then listened as they halted in the doorway. He didn't doubt for a minute that Dillon was trying to take in the disaster Hunter had created in such a small amount of time.

He heard a small but genuine chuckle in Dillon's question. "What happened?"

"I can't fucking cook," Hunter snarled. "In fact, I hate cooking. How about we go out instead? If this tastes half as bad as it smells, I'll be calling for an ambulance for the both of us."

Dillon came up behind him and wrapped his arms around Hunter's waist. His aroma had the same reassuring masculinity Hunter had loved about him the very first time he came fresh from the shower and took Hunter to bed.

Dillon chuckled again as he rubbed the stubble of his unshaven cheek against Hunter's. "How about I cook while you grab a shower?"

"But I wanted to treat you," Hunter said with a small frown.

"You can treat me some other way."

"That bad?" Hunter asked.

"Let's just say I can see all the love you tried to put into it."

Hunter laughed and turned in his arms so they were face to face. He took Dillon's waist in his hands. He could feel a pair of his own boxers and a t-shirt which Dillon had taken from his dresser, but he was otherwise unclothed. Arousal suddenly started growing in the pit of his belly, but he pushed it down and decided not to let it come to the surface. "You're pretty smooth, you know that? All the love I put into it?"

"They call it diplomacy," Dillon answered with a smirk.

"Slick is what I call it, but you're on. You make something edible and I'll take a shower. Maybe you'll let me take you out for dinner later."

"No work today?"

"No, it's an off day," Hunter answered.

"You called Margie and canceled, didn't you?"

"Does everyone understand my actions so easily? Yeah, I canceled," Hunter replied, dropping his head and resting it against Dillon's chest. "I thought we could use some time together...if you want," he added as he pulled back a little.

Dillon pulled him close again and squeezed as his chest filled with air. "You're exactly what I need right now. Thanks. And thanks for all your messages and texts. They got me through the last few days. Just knowing you were there for me to come back to."

Hunter pecked him on the cheek and turned for the shower as Dillon released him. He'd thought his messages would look like a desperate plea which he'd be ashamed of later. But he was glad they'd helped.

He heard Dillon chuckle as he looked around the kitchen again and smiled to himself. Lydia had explained many years ago, during a friend's funeral, that the best way to help someone through their grief was to make them feel useful and keep them busy. If nothing else, Dillon could certainly be helpful when it came to Hunter's kitchen. He hated the goddamned room with a passion.

"Hunter."

Hunter turned back to him.

"Let's do Thanksgiving at your mom's, if she still wants me."

"She does," Hunter answered. He knew that anyone he brought to her house would be welcome.

"Good."

"What about Travis?" Hunter asked.

Dillon tilted his head back and stared at the ceiling. "I'm sure the conversation will be intense, but it's time I face it. With you there…" he let the sentence fade away as he brought his gaze back to Hunter.

"I'll stomp him," Hunter said with a smile.

Dillon chuckled again, a soft reverberation deep in his chest which told Hunter he'd heal with time. "Yeah, that too."

Hunter smiled and turned for the shower. He had to remember to give his mom a call and let her know things were likely to be strained. But maybe, if he and Dillon were lucky, they could work through this and have a better time when they celebrated Christmas next month.

Chapter 7

They spent the next few days huddled around each other, entwining their bodies like they did their fingers. The gentle touch of skin was never more than a few paces away and it kept them close and always caressing each other with soft, languid strokes. The sex was sincere and wholesome and passionately hot – not erotic, but intense and filled with emotion.

Hunter worked from his desk while Dillon ran home, grabbed more clothes, and came back. He was concentrating at his desk when he felt Dillon come up behind him and caress his shoulder. He stopped the program and took off his headphones.

"You're freaking amazing on that thing," Dillon said. "How do you go so fast?"

"The screen reader," Hunter informed him with a shrug. "I'm wired differently and I don't have all the distractions you have. It reads what's on the screen and because I've been blind my whole life I can absorb what it says faster than you or probably any other sighted person could read it."

"Is that how you work on the voices for the books?"

"No, it's entirely different."

"Tell me," Dillon urged as he leaned down and kissed Hunter's temple.

Hunter curled into Dillon's kiss and reached an arm up to

hold him and kiss him fully on the lips. He loved the idea that Dillon was here constantly, but he could also feel his restlessness beginning to grow. From his perspective, it seemed as if Dillon was feeling a little trapped but hadn't quite figured that out yet. He needs something for himself, Hunter thought. It was a whisper of edginess Hunter was detecting at the moment, but it was something which would grow if Dillon didn't find his own outlet.

"When I'm creating an audio book, I'm manipulating sound," Hunter explained. "I'm not absorbing, but projecting; trying to get people to react to the nuances I hear in inflection and tone. Since they're not reading it, I'm attempting to draw on their cognitive associations by sound. Listen," he unhooked his headphones and pulled up an audio program he used in production work. "Close your eyes," he told Dillon.

Dillon closed his eyes and stood with his hand on Hunter's shoulder.

"Listen," Hunter said again. "Some people can only control and modulate their voice when singing, or at least that's the only time they think about it. When I go looking for new talent, I'm not just looking for their sound but their ability to control their voice."

"Like a music producer would?" Dillon asked.

"Something like that, but the nuances have to be more in control," Hunter answered. "Here, this guy is a newbie. One of the voices we just picked up." He played the recording. "See how he struggles with it? He's got potential, but he doesn't realize it yet."

"I don't hear it," Dillon admitted. "It sounds like a guy reading a story."

"You will. Listen to this one, same story, different speaker." Hunter played the second file and Dillon listened to the voice which was obviously different from the first one. Then, with Hunter's guidance, he tuned into the man's annunciation, inflection, tone, and harmony with what he was reading. All separate and distinct, but blended in the final product. Those subtleties made him pay closer attention to the words. Hunter smiled when he noted how Dillon's grip on his shoulder changed. He'd been pulled into the storytelling without even realizing it.

"Now here is the second guy's original read," Hunter said, playing a third recording.

"I hear it," Dillon said, seeming a little surprised. "It's probably not like you, but I understand the difference now."

Hunter clicked it off. "It's more subliminal than anything. You noticed it because I told you what to look for. What I'm attempting to do is evoke emotion through auditory input. Not just the spooky music crap, but changing people's reactions with variations in sound and vocalization. If it's done right, it will physically alter the chemistry in the brain, but on a really, really small level."

"That's…way more than what I thought you were doing," Dillon confessed.

Hunter shrugged. "Yeah, I know. Most people believe we just have a few schmucks reading the books we put in front of them, but they can't figure out how our sales keep growing. It's a science."

"Real science?" Dillon asked.

"Yes, real science," Hunter reaffirmed when he heard the skepticism in Dillon's voice. "Your hearing is hardwired right into the thalamus and cortex so your emotional processing can change according to outside auditory stimulation."

"Like the music just before a scene in a scary movie."

"Sort of, but that's a pretty unsophisticated level," Hunter said. "It has the same premise, but it's not quite what we do. If Hollywood really dug into this, they'd see they could go to an entirely cerebral level and then people would really be shitting their pants in the theater."

Dillon quickly knelt and gave him a peck on the cheek. "You amaze me, you know that?"

Hunter turned and beamed at him. Margie knew his secret, of course, but he'd never really had anyone appreciate his work like Dillon had just done. But then he never had anyone to talk to about it either. "Thanks."

"Can you take a break?" Dillon asked

"Now?"

"Never mind, if you're busy…" Dillon said as he stepped back and turned to leave.

Hunter reached out for him, found his leg and followed it up until he'd put his arm around Dillon's waist to draw him back. "I'm not busy," Hunter told him. "In fact, I need to take a break. What do you have in mind?"

"Well, it's nice out. I thought maybe we could have lunch at the little bistro again," Dillon offered.

"Our first date bistro?" Hunter asked.

"The same."

"Give me a minute. Do I look presentable enough for Atlanta company?"

Dillon bent down to nibble on his ear for a moment before he answered. "You'd look presentable in skid-marked underwear and stinky old socks," he whispered.

Hunter laughed. "God, let's hope it never gets that bad. If it does, you have permission to put me out of my misery."

***

The bistro was quiet. It was a little after lunch, but well before dinner. Dillon explained how they'd changed the artwork and how it gave the place a different feel. "Slightly more trendy," he said as he looked around.

"Can't tell," Hunter responded with a smile. It smelled the same, the acoustics hadn't changed, and it still offered the same clean, tactile sensation it had on their first visit.

The manager came by the table and seemed genuinely happy that they'd returned. He was even more ecstatic when Dillon told him they'd had their first date here. Hunter thought they were probably remembered because he was one of the few, if not only, blind patrons the restaurant had seen, but he said nothing.

"Connie must be missing me," Hunter said when the manager walked away.

"Connie?"

"The waitress who was drooling over you at the Rat Hole," Hunter explained.

"We could've gone there."

"No," Hunter answered. "I like this. It's...our spot."

Dillon reached over and traced a line across the tops of his knuckles with his fingertip. "I could get used to making a lot more spots for us."

"I could too," Hunter admitted.

"I've been thinking..."

Hunter waited for more, but it didn't seem to be coming. "About?"

Dillon hesitated and seemed unable to express his thoughts. "These last few days...I'd like things to be like...kind of...permanent, or at least semi-permanent."

Hunter's heart did a little flutter and his mind went blank almost instantly. "I..." The words were wrapped up in his mouth and wouldn't come out. "What are you trying to say?"

"I want you to move in with me," Dillon said as he grabbed Hunter's hand and held it in his own in the middle of the table. "And I already know all the arguments. Everyone will claim it's too fast, but I want you more than a few hours a day."

Hunter could feel the tension of his question build in Dillon's grip as the silence stretched between them. He hadn't expected this and didn't know how to answer. "I...I don't what to say."

Dillon released his hand and went to pull it back across the table, but Hunter snatched it back and put his own grip on it. He wasn't willing to let Dillon close him off because he didn't get the immediate answer he was looking for.

"I'm going to be completely honest here," Hunter said. "I care about you, a lot. I hope you know that. I mean really understand. But I don't think moving in is a good idea yet."

"Why not?" Dillon asked. Hunter heard him try to swallow the pain in his voice, but he had to be truthful about this. He'd already come way too close to losing Dillon because of rash decisions in the last few days and he wasn't about to do it again if he could help it.

"Well…" This was going to be harder than he thought. "You've still got things to work through with your family, and I'll be there to support you every step of the way," Hunter said. "But beyond that, what are you going to do with yourself?"

"You mean money?" Dillon asked.

Hunter heard the confusion in Dillon's question. He thought he was being rejected and was searching for a reason why in Hunter's response.

"I've got plenty of that," Dillon said.

"No, Dillon. I mean you. What's going to make you happy? I can already feel your restlessness with me in the apartment. You're antsy. How long do you really think you'll be amused by standing over my shoulder watching me work?" Hunter asked pointedly.

"Am I bothering you? You don't want me there?"

Hunter squeezed his hand again and brought his other hand

up to the table and put it on top, holding Dillon's hand in his own and rubbing it with his fingers. "That's far from what I want or mean, and I think you know it. I want you to be happy when you're with me. I want to know how I can make it happen for you."

"I want to be with you," Dillon argued. "That's all I need."

Hunter smiled. "And I want to be with you too. Very much. But if we're talking long-term you need to find something for yourself that isn't me. Does that make sense?"

"Like a job?" Dillon asked. "Is that what this is about?"

"A job, a passion, a hobby, whatever you want to call it, but something that's all you; something we can celebrate together," Hunter offered.

"I've been thinking about going back to school, getting a degree maybe. I don't know in what. Roland kept suggesting it, but…" he shrugged and Hunter could hear how he was still grasping for answers. "I just never got to it," Dillon continued. "I got my GED. It was one of Roland's requirements."

"That's a start."

"So if I go to college you'll move in with me?" Dillon asked.

"No, that's not what I'm saying." He cut his words short. Dillon was still reeling from his answer and he had to make it clear to him what he was trying to say. This wasn't a litmus test he was proposing. "I want you to find something that's all yours which nobody, not even me, can take from you. If you don't have something that's just yours, we won't ever be able to survive. I'm a realist, Dillon, and I do want you in my life much more than you have been. But I don't want it to crumble in three months because you haven't found your own space yet. You told me yourself, you're not quite comfortable in your condo. How long would it be before you felt crowded?"

Dillon pulled his hand away again and this time Hunter let it go. He could feel Dillon's sentiment wash over him from across the table. He didn't need his sight to see it. Dillon felt hurt and betrayed.

"That's because I'm there alone," Dillon stammered. "It's like a museum. All you have to do is say no if you don't want to move in. You don't have to get all psychoanalytic on me."

"But I do want to move in, Dillon. That's the problem. I'm trying to throw some rationality into it before we jump in and then have nothing in three months."

"You do? Want to, I mean." Dillon asked, a mellowed enthusiasm creeping back into his voice.

"Yes, I do, just not yet," Hunter said. "Not for the reasons everyone else would claim, but because I do care, and I do want it, and for more than a few months. But there are some logistics we'd have to work out too. My apartment is also my office, so there's that and the individual needs I have."

"Whatever it is, I'll take care of it," Dillon said immediately.

Hunter felt Dillon's fingers wrap around his hand again.

"Is there a timetable with this rationality?" he asked.

The first thing that ran through Hunter's mind was that they'd wait until Dillon had made a decision about how he was going to deal with his mother. No matter how hard it was, Hunter knew he couldn't put himself between the two. If he did, he'd risk becoming the reason they didn't come back together. He'd fight for Dillon, but he couldn't be the cause for Dillon's permanent separation from his family. In the end, it would kill anything he and Dillon built together.

"No timetable," Hunter answered, "Just a known eventuality. And if we're moving my office…" He thought the absolute truth would serve them best. "If we're moving my office, which is my livelihood, then we have to know this is something we both want. I can't have whimsy affecting my business. Otherwise, I'll be back at my mom's house if something goes wrong, and that is so not happening."

Dillon's mood shifted dramatically, coming close to what it was when they first sat down. Hunter felt his body relax as the tension of the conversation fled once more.

"I guess I can live with that, for now," Dillon said. "And I promise, no matter what happens, I'm not going to send you back to your mom's." He chuckled.

"And in the meantime?" Hunter asked.

Their lunch came and interrupted the conversation. Dillon fell into relative silence while they ate. He made quiet comments about the food and traded banter with the staff, but Hunter suspected he might have been giving deeper consideration to his question. The manager came around again, as did the waitress, and by the time they finished they were both ready to leave, feeling a little over attended to by the staff. Their assurance that they'd return garnered a sincere thanks as they left.

"Want to go for a walk?" Dillon asked as the door to the restaurant closed behind him.

"A walk?" Hunter asked.

"Yeah, Piedmont Park is just down the street."

"Sure," Hunter answered. He'd walked it several times with his guide when he first moved to Atlanta. He remembered that, during those walks, he'd questioned whether he'd ever find himself there with someone he cared about. Back then, he'd doubted the eventuality, but now he smiled to himself, realizing how much his life had changed in the last few months.

***

"Have you ever been up north during the winter?" Hunter asked as he held Dillon's arm and let him lead as they made their way down the walkway by Oak Hill. The wind was picking up and getting brisk. Hunter leaned into him, resting his head on Dillon's shoulder for a moment.

"No," Dillon answered. "Why do you ask?"

"Winter smells so good. I think that's what I've always loved about the holiday season, you know?" He was feeling… What was he feeling? Weird. It was the first word that came to his head. He was feeling full, and alive and wanted. He squeezed Dillon's hand, raised his head, and let Dillon resume their walk.

How long has it been since you allowed anyone to lead you? he asked himself. He really couldn't remember a single time other than when he worked with a sighted guide, and even then he hadn't allowed the man to take control. Was Dillon taking control? Or was he letting all his old barriers down and letting Dillon in?

"What aroma defines the season for you?" Dillon asked.

"Hmm, tough one. There's the bite in the cold, that ozone-chill smell. Then there's the wood smoke in the air, that's my favorite. I like the food of the season too — pumpkins and spices, cocoa, apple pie. I don't know if I could define it with a single odor. What about you?"

He felt Dillon shrug before he answered. "Not as pleasant as yours. There were a lot of times when different smells brought back memories I didn't want, especially when I was on the street," Dillon admitted. He said nothing more until Hunter nudged him with his elbow. "Cold cement," he admitted. "The dusty rock smell that seeps in behind the sinuses and just sits there until it's in your bones." He paused. "That's what stands out most."

"Why?" Hunter asked. He was suddenly sorry he'd prompted Dillon for an answer.

"It's what I remember just before Shu-shu found me. Not too much else, but that smell…" His voice tapered off with some unpleasant memory. "Sorry, like I said, not as nice."

Hunter pulled Dillon against him with a gentle tug on his arm and squeezed his hand, rejecting his apology. It was an odor Dillon equated with rejection and it would likely never leave him. "I'm sorry," Hunter said.

"Stop saying that," Dillon replied. "It's not your fault. Besides, it helps to let some of it out. You're the only person I've ever talked to about any of this."

"We can talk anytime you want," Hunter offered.

"Who wants to be a downer all the time?" Dillon said. "I'm tired of finding all these persistent reminders in my life." He chuckled before he continued. "Which is probably why I sounded so pathetic asking you to move in. I guess I thought you could help me change that. I didn't mean to sound like I was pressuring you, it just…" he shrugged and went silent.

Hunter squeezed his hand. He didn't have to finish the sentence. Hunter knew what he meant. It was a feeling of completeness as if you had found and filled the elusive hole in your life. It was exactly how he felt about Dillon.

"Soup," Hunter announced as they rounded the corner by the botanical gardens.

"Huh?"

"When I was little my mom used to make this soup with sweet potatoes and Andouille sausage. She'd only make it in the winter because it was so thick and heavy. But it was sweet and spicy and smoky. That's what winter makes me think of – ozone outside in the cold and her soup inside the house."

Dillon smiled and looked at him. "Soup."

Hunter chuckled. "Soup."

"Will she be making it for Thanksgiving?" Dillon inquired.

"Don't think so. She hasn't made it in years. I don't know what made me think of it."

"Maybe I'll ask her for the recipe."

"Could you make it?" Hunter asked in surprise.

"I don't see why not. I don't think I could make it in your kitchen, though."

"Why not?"

Dillon chuckled. "Because my love, I'm sure I would need more than a can opener and a microwave."

Hunter laughed. "Hey, I can make a wicked sandwich."

"I know," Dillon said with a groan. "I know."

Hunter laughed again and gave him a quick elbow. "Just for that when I move in, you're doing all the cooking."

"Deal," Dillon quickly agreed.

"Uh," Hunter grunted, voicing his faux indignation. He laughed and squeezed Dillon's hand again. "What would you like for Christmas?" he asked after they had walked in silence for a few minutes.

"You."

"You already have that," Hunter answered with a smile. "Really, what would you like?"

Dillon stopped and pulled Hunter to him. "I don't want anything else. I just want to be happy with you."

Hunter could feel the blush run up to his face. "My mom's going to ask me," he said quietly, relishing how the cold November air carried Dillon's warm aroma to him. He could almost taste the fragrance of his masculine skin.

"I'll tell her the same thing," Dillon said.

Hunter heard footsteps approaching, two sets almost

synchronized in their walking. "So cute," he heard one of them say.

"Is that about us?" he asked Dillon.

"Yes, we seem to be attracting a crowd."

"We are?"

"Well," Dillon observed as he glanced around. "There are quite a few eyes following us."

"Why, they've never seen a blind man?" Hunter questioned him. He could feel his aggression pop into its old posture of hostile defensiveness.

Dillon kissed him before he could go on. When Hunter melted into the kiss, he pulled back. "My little ninja," Dillon smiled. "They just want to be where I am. No harm intended."

Hunter shrugged and lost his hostility in Dillon's quiet passion. From his experience with the gay men of Atlanta, he thought they were looking at Dillon more than him, but he appreciated the thought. "Habit," he said of his sudden demeanor.

"I think I'm going to go home tonight and give you some space," Dillon announced.

Hunter stopped suddenly and jerked Dillon's arm back, turning him so they were face to face. "That's not what I meant in the restaurant. It's not space I want…" Hunter said as he reached up and captured the side of Dillon's face in his palm. He ran his thumb across Dillon's chin, feeling the small stubble. "…It's breadth, and the strength between us to know that we're ready for the next step. I want to do it this way so it lasts, and I need you to understand that for me."

"I understand."

"Do you?" Hunter asked. "Then why do I still hear rejection in your voice?"

"Because I'm impulsive and immature, and…in love with you."

Hunter's mouth opened, but no words came out. Dillon chuckled and lifted his chin, closing Hunter's mouth for him. "That's probably much too soon to say, but there it is," Dillon told him.

Hunter gripped his cane a little tighter, feeling himself fill with emotion. But he still wanted to stick to his argument. They had to wait, it was too soon.

"Should I take your silence as rejection?" Dillon asked, teasing him.

Hunter shook his head. "No, it…You caught me off guard."

"Ah, so now I know what it takes to get your guard down," Dillon whispered, the humor in his voice a small snigger at Hunter's expense.

Hunter opened his mouth again, but Dillon put his finger over it to stop him. "You don't have to say anything. In fact, I'd rather you didn't. Okay?"

Hunter nodded. He didn't know what he was going to say anyway, he was just catching flies. He snapped his mouth closed and nodded a second time.

Dillon stepped to his side and Hunter slipped his hand back into the crook of his arm, letting Dillon lead as they walked the rest of the way around the park.

"Could you stay just one more night?" Hunter asked above the discreet whispers of other couples and the laughter of the children moving around them.

"I could, but why?"

"I don't want to let you go just yet. Is that enough of a reason?" Hunter asked.

Dillon squeezed his hand, telling Hunter it was more than enough. They crossed over the bridge on the lake and started to make their way back to his apartment. The quiet settled between them and the crisp November air brought a familiar longing.

"What?" Hunter asked when he heard Dillon emit a small sigh from beside him.

"I was just thinking about the cabin…and the rain."

Hunter smiled, wondering how Dillon had matched his own thoughts so perfectly. "But it's not raining."

He squeezed Hunter's hand. "We'll make up for it, somehow."

Chapter 8

By the time they got back to the apartment, the quiet sentiment of the rain was forgotten. It had become cold and blustery outside and they needed heat. Small touches had grown frantic in the November wind, a caress was filled with scalding anticipation, and even the staccato of Hunter's cane tapping against the pavement accentuated their savage longing.

Hunter turned and shoved Dillon against the wall as soon as he closed the door. He loved his hard body, the way he smelled, the curve of his shoulders when he wrapped his arms around him, the firm flesh of his ass in his hands when he fucked him. He mashed his face to Dillon's pouty lips and crammed his tongue into Dillon's mouth. When he pulled away, he bit Dillon's lower lip just hard enough to draw blood. He pulled his coat off and tossed it further into the apartment as he waited for Dillon's reaction.

"Hsss," Dillon hissed. He wiped his mouth with the back of his hand and saw a small spot of blood. He looked at Hunter in shock.

"Think you can handle this?" Hunter asked.

Dillon jerked his coat off, threw it on the floor, and drove Hunter back against the other wall. A picture clattered to the floor as he pressed against him, his bloody lip firm and hard against Hunter's mouth.

Hunter reached down and found Dillon's cock growing hard and pressing against his pants. He dug his fingers into it, clutching it through the fabric with a forceful stroke. Dillon let out a low agonized groan.

He rolled his head back and Dillon moved to his Adam's apple, laving his neck and sucking his way down. His touch was like liquid sugar; sweet, and hot, and running so slowly over Hunter's skin that it felt like he was on fire every time Dillon caressed him with his lips.

"You are so fucking hot," Dillon murmured into his neck. He pushed Hunter's shirt up so he could get to the skin and ran his hands across the hard muscle of Hunter's chest.

Hunter's back arched and he gasped as Dillon's cold fingers grabbed his nipples. They became erect in an instant and Dillon pinched one hard as he pushed Hunter's shirt above his head with his free hand.

Dillon licked one nipple slowly, circling with his tongue before he puckered and took it into his mouth. Hunter's breath caught as he sucked. The heat from Dillon's lips and the flickers from his tongue sent shivers down Hunter's spine. His other nipple was pulled and twisted in Dillon's cold fingers.

Dillon switched his mouth and hand and Hunter's breath stuttered as his nipples came alive with the sensations.

He grappled with his shirt, pulled it from around his wrists, and threw it into the room. He needed his hands on Dillon. He needed to touch him and feel him and smell him. He needed the strength of Dillon's body as the ache inside him grew and became a hunger.

He ran his hands through Dillon's hair and smelled the cold November air still trapped in it. Dillon slowly pulled Hunter's zipper down and reached inside to grab at his hard, hot cock while he continued to suckle on his tits.

When Dillon grabbed his shaft and squeezed, Hunter struggled for breath at the hard viciousness of his hold. He took it from the root and drew up – a firm, solid grip that pulled and stretched his shaft. He stroked up and down and slowly dragged his thumb across Hunter's sensitive head, rubbing the pre-cum in a small circle and making Hunter cry out loud.

Hunter thrust his pelvis out and moaned when Dillon snaked his hand deep into his pants and cupped his balls with his cold fingers. He stood on tiptoes trying to get away, trying to reject the frigid ecstasy he felt as Dillon rolled and kneaded his nuts.

He bit his lower lip and felt the pressure grow in his balls as his breath became heavy. He needed to cum and he could feel his reason flee only to be replaced by the hard, hot lust that had brought him and Dillon together in the beginning. The beginning Hunter thought irrationally. It seemed like years ago; decades since this man touched his body and made it sing.

Dillon stood up fully and gently grabbed the back of Hunter's head. He pulled Hunter's lips to his own and thrust his tongue into Hunter's mouth, waiting for him to take it; waiting for him to push it out and offer his own.

"So freaking hot," Dillon murmured when he pulled away and looked at the raw hunger in Hunter's face. He kissed him again and dropped down to his knees, stripping Hunter's pants and boxers to his ankles.

Hunter gasped as Dillon closed his mouth around the head of his cock and worked his lips down to the root. What the fuck is wrong with me? he asked himself. He was ready to blow his load like he was getting his very first blowjob.

"Stop," Hunter begged. "You're going to make me cum."

Dillon smiled around him as his body tensed. He redoubled his efforts and used Hunter's ass as a grip. He hammered Hunter's cock deep into his own throat.

There was no way Hunter could hold back under the assault, his whole body was like a circuit and the only place he was plugged into was Dillon's hot mouth. He gritted his teeth, grabbed Dillon's head, and jabbed his cock in. He came. Four heavy bursts coated Dillon's throat before he pulled back and finished by spraying across Dillon's hot tongue.

Dillon savored the prize. He nursed the last few drops from Hunter's sensitive cock and then rose to his feet, joining Hunter's lips and thrusting his tongue into his mouth again. He let Hunter taste his own cum, let him share in the small victory he just claimed. Hunter sucked on him hungrily, feeling himself become hard again at Dillon's insistent advance.

Dillon pressed him to the wall, pushed him flat. His hands came up on both sides of Hunter's head and he continued to drive his tongue into Hunter's mouth with a furious need.

"I'm going to fuck you raw," Dillon rasped when he pulled away.

Hunter nodded. He wanted to be fucked. He wanted to be fucked hard. He wanted to feel Dillon pounding his ass into the mattress. He ached for the heat of it. His ass was an empty vessel waiting to be filled with Dillon's throbbing, merciless cock. This would be payback for the bloody nip he took. "Yes."

He barely had the word out before Dillon bent down and scooped him into his arms. He yanked Hunter's pants from his ankles with one hand and carried him into the bedroom.

Hunter felt Dillon watching as he put him on the bed, his gaze hungry and a raw, almost physical touch. Dillon pulled his clothes off and tossed them to the floor.

Hunter could hear Dillon stroking himself. He spread out on the bed, lifted his knees, and exposed his aching hole. He was waiting.

Dillon growled; a low lust-filled rumble which came up from the pit of his stomach and set Hunter's longing completely on edge. In that snarl, he heard the roughness of Dillon's hands as they caressed him; the hard steel of his arms when they began to enclose him, and the animal need Dillon had to be buried inside Hunter's hot ass. Hunter wanted him so desperately he thought he'd scream.

With one hand, Dillon grabbed his ankle and flipped Hunter on his stomach as if he only had the weight of a small child. He jumped on his back and pushed all his weight down on Hunter's shoulders, forcing him into the mattress. He lined his cock up, swiped it once across Hunter's hot entrance and then sat up on his haunches, stealing the prize Hunter wanted so desperately.

He forced Hunter's legs open further, looked down at his quivering ass and shoved two fingers in deep. Hunter shrieked under their touch; his cold, rude digits penetrating him and making him howl as every muscle in his body went taut.

He writhed and bucked, but Dillon held him firmly. He jammed his fingers in and spread them as he worked Hunter's asshole. When he pulled them out, he licked each finger and shoved them in again, pushing them further, adding more fingers until he was almost fisting him.

"Please," Hunter gasped. "Please. It hurts," he whimpered. He'd never been fisted before and the pain was excruciating. Dillon withdrew his hand and slapped his ass hard.

He crawled back on him, lined his cock up once again, and stopped.

Hunter was whimpering under him, but he wanted it so desperately. He reached back to urge him on, but Dillon slid down and gently lifted Hunter's hips. He began slowly and softly licking Hunter's anus like he was trying to apologize with his tongue.

Hunter grabbed a pillow, buried his face in it and screamed. He couldn't help it. Dillon's tongue was so hot and long and wet against him he was ready to cum again. His cries grew louder and became an inarticulate warble into the pillow as Dillon tongue-fucked him to senselessness. And just when he thought he couldn't take another swipe Dillon sat up, leveled his cock, and rubbed it up and down Hunter's slick hole.

He just kept rubbing and rubbing…sliding his cockhead slowly up and down across Hunter's sensitive hole until Hunter couldn't stand it anymore. He was squirming on the bed, begging him to put it in. He needed Dillon in him. He wanted Dillon to be buried up to his balls, and he wanted to be filled with his hot cum. "Please," he begged. "Please."

He had to get it inside. He wanted to feel those thick veins pulsing within him. He could hear Dillon's labored breathing and the need that went with it. He wanted Dillon buried in him; wanted to feel every ounce of his cock moving inside, touching the spot that only Dillon had ever reached.

He clenched his cheeks involuntarily and cried out when Dillon suddenly thrust his cock in. It made the pain that much sharper and that much more delicious. In a moment, the sting was gone and replaced by a throbbing whine. He didn't realize it was coming from his own mouth until Dillon halted his motion, reached over the side of the bed, and stuffed a sock in it.

"Quiet, boy," he commanded before he began ramming his cock into him.

Hunter moaned. He bucked his hips back and pulled Dillon's cock further inside, the muscles of his ass gripping Dillon as he pulled out on the backstroke. He reached behind him and pulled his cheeks apart, exposing his hole, making it ripe for abuse. He wanted to draw Dillon forward so he could slam his ass back and bury

Dillon as far as he'd go.

Hunter thought that if he could just turn over and face Dillon, he could throw his legs in the air and expose himself so he could meet Dillon's thrusts. He went to roll, but Dillon wouldn't let him. He held him pinned with his ass poked into the air and his hands exposing his hole.

"Do you like that?" Dillon whispered with a harsh insistence.

Hunter knew he didn't want an answer. He was demanding his whimpers and moans, testing Hunter's flesh against the fat cock he had buried in his ass. Dillon wanted to know if he liked being fucked hard.

Hunter could only whine and nod. The sock in his mouth wouldn't let him speak. His blindness wouldn't let him meet Dillon's eye and beg for more. His tongue couldn't taste their sweat as they worked themselves into a hot frenzy.

"Take. That. Cock." Dillon ordered as his body tensed and his thrusts matched the staccato of his words.

Hunter moaned when he felt Dillon flood into him. He pushed himself back, milking Dillon's shaft, squeezing his muscles and relaxing them as he massaged Dillon for every single drop of cum he could get.

Dillon let go of his wrists and Hunter snatched the sock from his mouth and threw it across the room. "Again," he demanded, pushing his ass back against Dillon, willing him to become erect again.

Dillon fell forward and grinned against his back with a dark humor. Hunter waited motionlessly. In a moment, Dillon caught his breath, turned him over, and lifted his legs into the air.

Dillon's semen dripped from his ass when he pulled out. But Hunter wanted it again, and again, and again. He wanted this man inside of him, loving him, fucking him like a cold and dirty whore. That was the smell of winter; that was what he'd been searching for in the park. The hot stink of sweaty sex against the cold dark of the room.

Goddamn, he loved sex with this man.

***

It was morning. They were both raw. Hunter could think of no other word to explain it. The sex had been hard and rough and exquisite. It felt like his ass had been mauled, but he couldn't wait to do it again. He ran a finger lightly through the rough scratch of Dillon's beard. Then traced it along his nose, over his eyebrows, down along the sides of his head, which brought him back to Dillon's lips; those soft, soft lips. Lips he wanted to kiss; lips which were smiling now; lips that held an easy grin.

"Sorry," Hunter said as he pulled his hand away.

"For what?"

"Waking you."

"I was awake."

Hunter smiled and traced the outline of his face again. "Liar," he said quietly.

"Are you memorizing my face?" Dillon asked.

Hunter shook his head. "No. I did that the first night. I just wanted to touch you again...make sure you're real."

Dillon pulled him close and kissed him softly. "As real as it gets."

"It's so different from what I imagined."

"What's that?" Dillon asked.

"You...us." Hunter shrugged. "I don't know...but not this, not...you," he offered, grasping for his words. "I guess my imagination wasn't as cracked up as it was supposed to be. It fell pretty short."

"Is that a good thing?" Dillon asked.

Hunter nodded and met his lips. It was an excellent thing and words would only spoil it.

Chapter 9

"Are you ready for this?" Dillon asked as they drove to Lydia's house.

"Are you?" Hunter responded. They hadn't brought a thing for Thanksgiving. Lydia had insisted they bring nothing but a change of clothes if they were going to stay the night, but Hunter had immediately nixed the idea. If things went bad with Travis, he wanted a quick escape to his apartment and not a lingering masquerade filled with tension in his old bedroom.

"I don't know," Dillon told him. "Travis and I didn't really talk much."

"Did you give him a chance to talk?" Hunter asked.

"Honestly, no. I wasn't in the mood for listening. I just wanted my dad's death verified. He had more to say but..." He shrugged his grief away. "And he was at work."

Hunter knew from his short choppy sentences that he'd probably still been in a state of denial when he spoke to Travis. He was having a hard time accepting it even now. He reached over and gave Dillon's leg a gentle squeeze. "We don't have to go, Dillon. I mean that."

"Of course we do. Your mom is expecting us. And don't all families drag all their old issues across the table during the holidays? Isn't it the reason everyone dreads going home?" he asked with a small but unconvincing laugh.

Hunter nodded. "You could be right." He only wanted the day over and had no plans to stay any longer than necessary.

"I'm not going to make a scene. I promise," Dillon said. "He's already told me the worst of it. What could be worse than my father died?"

Hunter shook his head without a reply. If there was something, he didn't want to know. Nor did he want Dillon exposed to it over dinner. "Mom wanted us to stay the night."

"So you said, but I didn't bring anything."

Hunter shrugged. "Me either. I told her I didn't want to."

"Why?" Dillon asked as a smirk came into his voice. "Is she going to put us in separate bedrooms so we don't do the nasty?"

"As if. We would not be fucking in my mom's house even if we were staying."

Dillon laughed. "You afraid she's going to hear you moaning?"

"Hell, yeah." He cringed at the thought. It was bad enough that he'd walked in on her and Travis, but the reverse… He'd never be able to return home. "I couldn't face her again."

Dillon laughed and grabbed Hunter's hand from his leg and slid it into his crotch as he drove. "How about if it's nice and slow – scorching hot, quiet sex?"

Hunter squeezed Dillon's crotch and moaned silently at the thought. "You just want to fuck me in my old bed, don't you?"

"Didn't you ever think about it when you were growing up?"

Dillon asked. "Some hot stud fucking your brains out in the bed you slept in as a teenager? I know I did."

"Can we get off this subject? You're making my dick hard." Hunter said as he pulled his hand back into his own lap.

"Ah-ha, so you did think about it!" Dillon quickly reached between Hunter's legs and squeezed his cock once. "Such a bad boy," he teased and laughed.

"You're the first person I ever brought home," Hunter admitted.

"Really? Hmm. Well, it's the first home I've been brought to as a free person too. So I guess we're even."

"Free person?"

"Not rented for the night," Dillon explained. "You know queens and their soirées. Holidays are a busy season. Lots of people feel lonely and a lot more go looking for someone to hang on their arm and show off."

Hunter frowned. "Do you miss it, the parties and stuff like that?"

"No," Dillon answered. "If you want the truth, I spent most of the time wondering what my family was doing and the rest of it trying to convince myself how much fun I was having. I've never really enjoyed the holidays. They've always been just another working day. That's why this will be so different. I just want to enjoy it."

"As a family…" Hunter thought out loud.

"You don't mind me latching on to yours, do you?" Dillon

asked.

"Of course not, I…kind of like the sound of it," Hunter admitted. "And you'll get to meet Toby and Garrett."

"Who are they?"

Hunter explained who they were and how they had been such a large part of his childhood. He also told Dillon about his mother's sudden change of heart when it came to them. He admitted he was still in shock over the invitation extended in their direction and was interested in seeing how things went. "I think it's your cousin's doing," he admitted.

"Travis?"

"Yeah, she's…changed. I don't know how to explain it any better. But she's a lot different from the woman I grew up with."

"In a good way?"

Hunter considered it for a moment. "In a more open way, I guess. It's hard to explain, but it seems pretty weird that you showed up in my life at the same time Travis turned up in hers."

"Yeah, it is. Maybe your family was meant to mend mine."

"Or just have great sex with them," Hunter said and started laughing.

**

Hunter heard Dillon let out a tightly controlled breath of resignation when he parked the car in front of Lydia's house. He reached over and took Dillon's hand. "We really don't have to do this. We can go home right now."

Dillon squeezed his hand. "We've come all this way, and

there's someone peeking out of the curtain. They already know we're here."

"I'll take the blame," Hunter suggested.

"No. We're going to do this and we're going to enjoy ourselves. If it gets too deep, I'll tell Travis to stow it until another day."

And push it all back down again, Hunter thought. "Okay, but promise me you'll let me know when you're ready to go."

Dillon leaned over and kissed him. "With those magic ears you'll probably know before I have to say anything."

Hunter shrugged. He could not deny how attuned he was to Dillon's voice already. If Dillon really understood how he subconsciously evaluated his breathing or all the little fidgeting sounds and tics he made, he'd probably freak out. It wasn't something Hunter did on purpose. It was how he processed the information which sighted people typically dismissed. "Occupational hazard," he told Dillon. "Ready?"

"Yeah, let's do this."

***

The tension in the house was a physical thing. Hunter felt it as soon as his mother opened the door. She greeted them both cordially and gave Dillon a hug, letting him know he was welcome and how happy she was that he'd decided to come. She went to put their coats away then told them to go into the living room with everyone else.

Toby came bursting around the corner when he heard

Hunter's voice and latched on to his arm. He began chattering about the turkey, how he was helping Miss Lydia, and how Christmas was coming. He didn't stop until Garret came into the foyer and made him give Hunter space to breathe.

Hunter chuckled. "He's okay."

"Just excited to see you again," Garret said. He lowered his voice, "And he's as surprised to be here as I am."

"Should've been years ago," Hunter whispered back to him.

"That's what your mom said too. That's why we came. I couldn't handle another apology."

"Garret, this is Dillon," Hunter said as Dillon began to fidget by his side.

"Nice to meet you," he heard Garret say as they shook hands.

"Likewise," Dillon offered.

"And this is Toby," Hunter said, listening to Toby's suppressed but still excited exhalations.

"Toby, that's me," Toby chimed.

Hunter smiled. Toby's introduction never changed. He'd throw his hand out, wrap his meaty paw around you and shake your arm off if you let him.

"Is Travis here yet?" Hunter asked.

"In the living room," Garret answered. "But I figured we'd meet you here and give Toby a little space to move around."

"She must have the tree up already," Hunter surmised.

"Yep," Garret answered. "And he'd have it on the floor in a minute in that little room."

"They got me presents," Toby exclaimed. His voice was beaming with anxious, childlike excitement.

"They did?" Hunter asked, genuinely surprised.

"Yep, it's a big box too. Miss Lydia says it's a big-boy present."

"Ooh," Hunter said. "Did you shake it yet?"

"Pappy won't let me." A frown curled his lips down. They all laughed at the disappointment in his voice.

"We'll do it later," Hunter whispered as if they were alone.

Toby clapped in excitement then ran into the kitchen to tell Lydia that he and Hunter would be shaking the present later.

"I thought you might," he heard her call from the kitchen.

He smiled. Guessing presents had become a contest between them many years back. The first time he guessed his Christmas presents was when he was about seven. He did it again the next year and then purposefully missed a couple the following Christmas because he noticed that Lydia seemed mildly upset over the fact that he had such great deductive powers. But it was a trick. The next year she made sure all the presents were securely wrapped and muted and he'd never guessed one correctly since.

"I hope you know what you just started," Garret chuckled. "Come on, she'll keep him busy in the kitchen. He's been helping her out since we got here. Game's on too."

Hunter marveled at his comment but said nothing. Lydia had made the kitchen a forbidden zone when he was as young as Toby was mentally. She'd all but outlawed the use of the stove until he was in his teens. Maybe it was why he loathed the kitchen so much now. "Game?" Hunter asked.

"Football, of course. Boy, you ain't changed none," Garret chuckled as he turned and ambled back to the living room.

Hunter groaned. Garret had tried and tried to get him interested in football when he was young, but it had never caught on. He couldn't see the players or the game and other than the grunts and groans of a tackle there wasn't much that interested him. He did remember a peculiar adolescent curiosity he'd had about what all those hot, sweaty men might smell like during sex. He also recalled wondering if their grunts and groans would match the same brutish staccato he heard just before the whistle blew. But that had been the extent of his interest.

He reached back for Dillon's hand and led the way into the living room. He stopped in the doorway. He heard the television blathering about the game but wasn't quite sure where Garret and Travis had seated themselves.

"Couch is open," Dillon whispered from behind.

Hunter knew this room and precisely how Lydia had set it up for Christmas. She did it the same way every year. The tree was in front of the bay window and she moved the television into the corner. The couch was directly across from tree and two chairs capped the ends of the room. It was just big enough when it was only the two of them, but he didn't doubt it would feel a little crowded today.

Lydia came bustling into the doorway just as he was about to sit down. "Dinner will only be a few more minutes. Garret, can you and Hunter come help me?" she asked before she disappeared again.

He felt Dillon squeeze his hand in quiet resignation. They had both hoped they could have dinner first and then allow Travis and Dillon time to speak alone. But it seemed Lydia had other ideas.

"It's okay," Dillon whispered in his ear.

"You sure?"

"I'm sure. Go help her out."

"Okay." He felt Dillon kiss his temple as Garret squeezed by.

"What's all that about?" Garret asked when they walked into the hall.

"Dillon and Travis are cousins, family issues," Hunter explained.

"Ah, well this should make for an exciting holiday then. Will there be fireworks too?" Garret chuckled.

Hunter didn't smile. "Hopefully not."

Chapter 10

"You plan that?" Dillon asked as he looked over at Travis.

"No," Travis answered. "She said she wasn't sure if you were coming."

Dillon moved to the chair at the opposite end of the room instead of sitting on the couch. "I wasn't sure I was coming. I didn't want to ruin their holiday with our problems."

"There's no problem here, Dillon. There never has been. I don't know what you told Hunter, but he seems to think I'm some kind of threat to you."

Dillon looked at him for a moment before he answered. Travis sat like a rigid little statue. He couldn't tell if it was a sense of haughtiness or worry that held him so still. "You're no threat to me, you or anyone else in our family. Not anymore," Dillon answered.

"Then why are you so mad at me?"

Dillon's jaw tightened. "Because you're a part of everything I want to forget and move beyond. You, your mother, my mom, and every hypocritical asshole in the town we grew up in."

"We used to be friends," Travis said.

"We did, but that time has passed."

"What did I do to you?" Travis demanded suddenly, his voice going up. "I was fourteen-years-old. What more do you think I could've done?"

Dillon's face went dead. "And how old are you now?"

"What?"

"Now, Travis, today. How old are you?" Dillon asked again.

"What the hell does my age have to do with it?"

He glared at Travis and felt his expression tighten. He didn't want to make this a full-blown confrontation, but he would if that's what Travis really wanted. "You could've come, or called…something. It would've been nice to know you gave a shit."

"Do you have any idea what they did to me after you left?" Travis asked. "They sent me off to Christian rehab and wouldn't let me out until they were convinced about how much I hated you. All because you left your fucking suitcase in my room. Four months I was locked in a goddamned room by myself while they tried to brainwash me."

Dillon didn't doubt anything about his aunt and uncle. They were the ones who brought his mother into the cult they called a church. He knew it was true. But four months wasn't ten years of sucking dick to survive. "I'm sorry to hear that, but that wasn't me."

"And it wasn't me who threw you out," Travis volleyed back at him with some anger. "You don't understand how hard it was for me to have to scream about how much I hated my faggot cousin, how he was going to burn in hell, all that ignorant shit. They took my cane and locked me in a room. Four months, and every single day the same questions about what we might've done together and how I felt about you."

Dillon's anger slipped. The tight knot he'd used for so many years to keep him warm was unraveling. "I'm sorry, Travis. I didn't even think about the suitcase."

"It's not about the fucking suitcase!" Travis yelled. "You were my best friend."

A silence settled between them as Dillon dropped his eyes to the floor. Words escaped him. There was only the noise of the television to fill the room.

"You're still my best friend," Travis said quietly. "That never changed."

Dillon looked up at him. "It's not that easy for me Travis, not by far. And if you really felt that way I don't think it would've taken Hunter and his mother for us to meet again."

"Your mother still wants to see you," Travis answered without responding to his accusation.

"I don't want to see her, ever."

"She's not going to stop until you see her at least once."

"And what's her excuse?" Dillon asked. "My name is in the phone book. All she had to do was look it up." But he already knew his mother's reason. She wanted him to come crawling back to her, to beg for her forgiveness and some Christian redemption he no longer believed in.

"Does she know we're in contact?" Dillon asked.

"No. They don't even know about Lydia yet. All they know is I met some girl," Travis informed him.

"Some girl?" Dillon repeated.

"Yes. Do you think they'll be any more receptive to Lydia than they were to you? She's older than my mom."

Lydia popped her head in the door and Dillon knew by the look on her face that she'd heard every word.

"Dinner's ready," she said with a smile which didn't quite reach her eyes.

"Okay, thanks," he said as he stood. Great, we're already ruining things for them, he thought as he watched her turn back to the kitchen.

"She heard that?" Travis asked.

"Yeah, she heard."

Travis blew out a long breath. "I should've skipped this," he said as he stood and grabbed his cane from where it was leaning against the chair.

"Why does she want to see me?" Dillon asked about his mother before he turned into the dining room.

Travis shook his head. "I don't know, but they think I'll be the first person you contact and I'm supposed to give you the message when it happens."

Dillon turned to go to the dining room and then stopped and looked back at him. "Why are you still there?" he asked Travis.

"Because, unlike you, I can't survive on the street. Otherwise, I probably would've taken off with you when you left," Travis answered.

Chapter 11

Dinner was a quiet affair and even though Lydia tried to keep an upbeat conversation going, the meal fell flat under the strain of the company. Even Toby noticed and sat with his head hung until Hunter reminded him that they had yet to shake his present.

After dessert, Garret announced it was time to take their leave and Toby and Hunter absconded to the living room and spent another twenty-five minutes shaking and guessing. But, as he assumed, Lydia had made sure there were no audible hints coming from the box.

Hunter finally admitted defeat. "Guess we'll have to wait until Christmas, buddy."

"Can I come back tomorrow and try again?" Toby pleaded.

Hunter laughed. He could hear the determination in his voice. He'd been just as resolute when he was a kid.

"I don't think Miss Lydia has time for that," Garret piped up from behind them. "Come on, Toby, time to go."

"You come back anytime," Lydia told Garret. "And be here on Christmas so Toby can open his present. We'll have dinner afterward." She handed him a couple of bags with leftovers from their dinner.

He nodded to her. "Thank you. Ready?" he asked Toby.

"Yeah," Toby sighed with regret.

Hunter listened as he worked his way around the room to say goodbye and smiled as he dragged his feet to the door to wait for Garret. He followed along behind and then met Garret on the porch with a handshake.

"That was nice," Garret said.

"Yeah fun, like a funeral," Hunter replied.

Garret chuckled. "It wasn't so bad, and your mom makes a mean plate. Better than anything I would've whipped up for us."

"I'll make sure to tell her," Hunter said. "You'll probably get a few more invites."

"She surprised me with this one," Garret admitted. "But Toby took right to her."

Hunter noted that the surprise in Garret's voice matched his own amazement. He shrugged. "Maybe it's the mom thing." She appeared to have taken to Toby just as readily and again he was sorry that it hadn't happened years ago.

"Maybe," Garret answered. "Nice out today, think I might take Toby to see his mama. We haven't been down to see her in a while."

Hunter nodded. He'd accompanied Toby and Garret to the cemetery twice over the years and both times had been as somber as their dinner had just been. Garret still pined for his wife and Toby had never known his mother so he didn't understand why they were visiting.

"Tell her I said hello," Hunter told him.

Garret shook his hand again. "I'll do that. Come on, Toby,"

he hollered, calling Toby back from the edge of the forest beside the house. "He wants to go exploring."

Hunter laughed. "We've talked about it enough."

"And that boy doesn't forget a thing," Garret said as Hunter heard Toby trotting over to them. "Go on and get in the truck," he directed Toby. "Take these," he added, handing him the bags Lydia had given him.

"Bye, Hunter. See you soon," Toby said.

"Bye." He put his hand out flat and gave Toby his goofiest wave. He heard him giggle and run over to the truck.

Garret was still beside him. "You know, he seems like a nice guy, Hunter. A little quiet, but friendly."

Hunter froze, the smile still plastered on his face. It was the first time Garret had ever openly acknowledged his sexuality. He'd never seemed homophobic, but he'd never acknowledged the topic either. "Thanks," Hunter answered, not quite sure how he should react.

He went back into the house when they left. He gave Dillon a squeeze on the shoulder as he sat back down and found out Lydia was making coffee. "What did you get Toby for Christmas?" he asked when she came into the living room.

"I'm not telling you," Lydia laughed. "You'll tell him for sure."

Hunter grinned. "Moi?"

"Coffee?" she asked.

The consummate host, Hunter marveled. They had lived an almost solitary existence during his youth and this was such a new side of her. He was actually beginning to enjoy it. "I'll take one."

"Just the two of us then," she said with a nod when Travis and Dillon both declined.

"On the porch," Hunter added as he stood back up again. "It's beautiful outside."

"You don't have to go," Dillon said, discerning Hunter's intent. "We're done talking."

Hunter hesitated for a moment. Travis hadn't said a word. Maybe they had more to talk about than Dillon realized. "Its okay, gives me some time to spend with my mom. Join us when you're done. Both of you," he added as he turned to the porch.

Chapter 12

"I don't think we have anything else to talk about," Dillon said after he watched Lydia go out the door with two mugs of coffee in her hand. She smiled at him momentarily and nodded. Dillon could see the origin of Hunter's smile on her face. She didn't realize it, but her smile, like Hunter's, gave him the confidence he needed in the decision he'd already made.

"I need to know what you want me to tell your mother," Travis said.

"Tell her not to bother me. That's what you can tell her. Tell her I'm not interested and tell her don't ever contact me."

"So you're just going to abandon her?" Travis asked.

"I can't believe you even asked me that fucking question," Dillon snapped at him. "Abandon her? She didn't even acknowledge me on my father's gravestone. Did you know that? It says loving husband, that's it. What the fuck do you think I owe her? I don't owe her a goddamned thing."

"So what do you want me to say?" Travis asked again.

"I don't want you to say shit. Nothing. There's no reason she'd ever make the jump from Lydia to me."

"She's been asking…"

"Tough shit!" Dillon yelled. He drew in a long breath and looked down the hall to see if his shouting had attracted attention. "My answer is final. I have no need to see her ever again. You can tell her that, or you can pretend we never met. I really don't give a shit either way. This conversation is done," Dillon said as he got up to leave.

"Maybe she doesn't want to be alone," Travis countered.

Dillon stopped in his tracks. "She doesn't want to be alone?" he asked, the venom rising in his voice. "I was alone for ten fucking years not knowing if I'd be alive the next day. That whole time she was praying to Jesus for what? My death? My redemption? What? You tell me. She can fuck off."

"And what about us?" Travis called after him.

Dillon stopped again and turned to look at him. He watched as Travis stood and searched the side of the chair for his cane. "I need some time," Dillon answered. "And I'm sorry about what you went through because of me. You know I never wanted it to happen." He turned to go out to the porch then stopped and turned back again. "I don't want Hunter or Lydia hurt because of what's between us, ever. They don't deserve it."

"Do you love him?" Travis asked.

"More than my own life," Dillon answered, "but I want him to understand just what that means before he says yes."

"Says yes to what?" Travis asked.

"Spending the rest of his life with me," Dillon said as he turned and went out to the porch.

Chapter 13

Lydia settled on the swing beside Hunter with two mugs in her hand. The scent of dark rum wafted up and he smiled. "Is this a celebration or just the good stiff one we need?"

"Both," Lydia laughed.

"Hmm, cinnamon," Hunter commented after he took a sip.

"I want you back for Christmas, both of you," Lydia said without hesitation.

"What about them?" Hunter asked, tilting his head back toward the house.

"Doesn't matter. You're my son. I want you home for Christmas."

"I don't want to ruin Christmas too."

"You didn't ruin anything," she admonished. "We both knew this was going to be difficult. By December," he felt the swing shift as she shrugged, "things may be different."

"And if not?"

"Well, it will be the three of us, and Toby and Garret."

"What about Travis?"

"Hunter, there's over thirty years between me and Travis. And you had plenty to say when I first told you how old he was. You think it hasn't crossed my mind too?"

"But that's not…"

"Hush."

He fell silent.

"Three decades is a long time, Hunter. It's a life full of time. You and Dillon have earned a right to enjoy what you have together…"

"And what about you?" Hunter interrupted. "What about you being happy? I'll admit I was shocked at Travis' age, but it also made me realize how much you gave up for me."

She waved his comment away. "I did what I had to do so we could survive, just like any mother would do. I've had my time, now it's your time."

"You sound like you're ready to pack it in and go live in the old fogey's home," Hunter complained.

She laughed lightly. "Not quite. But Travis does deserve someone around his own age."

"I think he should make that choice for himself," Hunter argued. "Don't you?"

He heard her take a sip of coffee without answering. Had he missed something? Were she and Travis arguing or was it just the tension of the day? She grew still beside him like she always did when she was upset and trying to shield him from something unpleasant.

"You deserve to be just as happy as I am," Hunter told her. "And if Travis is anything like Dillon," he added with a small hint of satisfaction in his voice, "I don't think he's going to give up so easy."

She kept quiet. Hunter knew she was holding back, but the

stubbornness he carried was a trait which came directly from her. She wouldn't discuss it with him no matter how much he insisted. It angered him sometimes, but that's just the way she was.

"Dillon wants me to move in with him," he said, changing the subject.

"Are you going to give up your apartment?" she asked in surprise.

He smiled at her astonishment. They'd had more than a few disagreements over his independence and his move to the city, so he wasn't surprised by her reaction. "Probably, but it won't be right away. I told him it was too soon and that he had to get things worked out with his family first."

"Good idea."

"Has Travis said anything about Dillon's mother? She wants him back."

"No, but a mother's pull is strong," she cautioned.

"So is his anger," Hunter said. He took another sip of coffee. "Do you think she could take him from me?" he asked, the worry still strong and hard against his heart. He wondered if that was the reason Dillon had so suddenly asked him to move in. Was it because he needed an anchor to keep him from returning home? Was he fighting against his mother's pull?

He felt Lydia's hand on his arm, a soft touch of reassurance. "I can't say for sure, but from the way he looks at you...I don't think it's something you need to worry about."

He let out a long breath, not realizing he'd held it while

waiting for her answer. He heard the door open and Dillon's footsteps as well as a cane tapping behind him.

"Everything okay?" Hunter asked.

"Yeah, we're okay," Dillon answered.

Hunter wasn't convinced. He heard the desire for it to be true, but not the belief. Like his mother, there was much more implied in the unspoken words. But maybe this was just a start. Maybe they had all expected a little too much from this day. It wasn't like ten years of animus was just going to vanish over a turkey dinner.

"Are you ready to go?" he asked Dillon.

"Are you?"

He handed Lydia his cup and stood up. "Yes, I hate driving at night. I can't see a damned thing." The joke fell flatter than he expected. "Coats?" he asked in the awkward silence which followed.

They said their goodbyes and headed home. Both he and Dillon were relieved that it was over.

Chapter 14

The following Monday, Dillon was standing at the stove in his condo when Hunter came into the kitchen. Dillon glanced over his shoulder, then had to do a double-take. Hunter just took his breath away – his fierce masculinity, his hard, dangerous hands, and the softness he kept hidden with his rare, but gently lopsided grin. Hair all mussed and standing in socks and boxers Hunter was even sexier, and so much more seductive. Dillon shook his head at the sight and had to smile and wonder, once again, how he'd ever been overlooked by anyone.

"I thought you were sleeping," Dillon said as Hunter came up beside him and nuzzled into his neck. Dillon tilted his head to the side, feeling the warmth of Hunter's sleep still radiating from his body.

"Uh-uh," Hunter murmured.

"I'm making you a spicy breakfast," Dillon insisted as Hunter reached down and began to paw at the front of the shorts he'd tossed on when he woke.

"Oh, good. I like spice in the morning."

Dillon pulled Hunter's hand away before it could creep into his shorts and lifted Hunter's chin to draw his face up and away from his neck. "Are you in withdrawal?" he asked. They hadn't had sex since Thanksgiving. He just hadn't been in the mood, and Hunter had been kind enough to give him some space. But apparently that space had now been reclaimed and filled with desire.

Hunter kissed him quickly, slipping his tongue into his mouth, tasting the coffee he'd brewed earlier as he sat and watched the sun come up.

"Yes, I need more. The spice must flow," Hunter quipped.

Dillon laughed. "You're completely impossible."

Hunter stepped back and let out a long sigh. It turned into a yawn with a lengthy stretch which ran from his toes to the hands he raised above his head as he twisted and turned his torso.

Jesus, Dillon thought as he watched his muscles firm. So fucking gorgeous.

"Okay," Hunter said covering his mouth to stifle the remainder of his yawn. "You convinced me. Coffee first, then the spice."

"Sit. I'll get it." Dillon kissed him and watched as Hunter traced his way around the counter and sat on the opposite side of the breakfast bar. He poured Hunter a cup of black coffee and pushed it across the counter. "Right in front of you," Dillon directed. "Careful, it's hot."

"What are you making? It smells terrific," Hunter asked after he took a sip of his coffee.

Dillon smiled. "There's just a little garlic sizzling in the pan. Is that what woke you?" He'd been up since five when the sun was still a whisper on the horizon.

Hunter had been spooned around him when he woke, but he still hadn't slept well. All night he kept rehashing the conversation he'd had with Travis on Thanksgiving. He couldn't forget the anguish he'd felt when he saw the inscription on father's gravestone. It had left a black residue within him that he hadn't been able to shake.

But that residue was diminished when he looked back at Hunter lying so peacefully in bed. He was all snug and cozy, and Dillon had wanted to crawl back in beside him. But he didn't, he came to the bed and kissed him on the temple instead. "I love you," he'd whispered.

"Mm, the garlic, yes. What are you making?" Hunter asked again.

"It's a recipe my…" He stopped and looked down at the ingredients he'd laid out. With a sudden flash saw his fifteen-year-old self standing in his parents' kitchen doing the same thing at four in the morning. The only difference was that it was his father sitting across from him, not Hunter, and they were getting ready to go out on a fishing trip.

"It's a recipe my dad showed me. Spicy sausages, eggs, peppers, and onions, and a bunch of other stuff." He shrugged the memory off with his words but even to him it didn't sound abandoned at all. "Thought it would be nice since it's so cold out today."

Hunter quietly put his coffee down and came around the counter again. He took Dillon's hand and started kissing each one of his fingers. He took each finger into his mouth and sucked it, licking each digit slowly.

"Are you trying to start something here?" Dillon asked as he watched Hunter casually make his way across his hand.

Hunter shrugged without releasing Dillon's finger. He wrapped his tongue around it and sucked hard as he slowly drew it out of his mouth. There was a small pop as he pulled it free and his lips smacked together. "The kitchen is a place to cook. Is it not?" he asked with a seductive purr.

Dillon stared at him as Hunter's lips opened slowly and took his finger again. He reached back and turned the burner off; pushing the sauté pan to the rear as he slowly pulled his finger out of Hunter's mouth. He took Hunter's head in his hands as his eyes closed and pulled Hunter to him.

"I don't think you know what you've started," Dillon said softly.

"Oh, I believe I do." Hunter smirked as he wrapped his arms around Dillon's shoulders and crushed their lips together.

Their kiss was soft and slow at first, then the heat set in and the fire of Dillon's lust opened. He clamped his hands on the thin boxers Hunter wore and kneaded Hunter's muscular ass through the fabric. He spread Hunter's cheeks as he massaged the firm flesh and slid his hand up and down his crack.

Hunter reached behind him, lifted Dillon's hands and shucked his boxers to the floor. He put Dillon's hands firmly back on his bare ass. "Why didn't you wake me?" he asked.

There was more to his question than the casual manner in which he asked, and Dillon saw that right away. "Because you looked too beautiful," he answered.

Hunter kissed him again and Dillon felt the warmth of the skin in his hands.

"I was already awake," Hunter whispered when he pulled away.

"You heard me?" Dillon asked, his body tensing. He was suddenly and irrationally afraid that he'd repeated I love you too soon for Hunter to accept.

In the park, those words had just slipped out of his mouth. And even though they were heartfelt, they seemed much more casual in that setting. That wasn't the case in the bedroom. This morning, his words had been drawn from the very deepest part of him. He'd left the bed feeling grateful for Hunter's presence in his life, but he also felt open and exposed. The raw tenderness he felt for the man sharing his bed still made him feel slightly vulnerable.

Hunter nodded silently in reply, the corner of his lip pulling in as he chewed on it. He said nothing more.

Dillon saw the apprehension in Hunter's face and quickly realized that he didn't have anything to fear. It wasn't the uneasiness of a mutual feeling which Hunter lacked, but a doubt which cautioned the speed of their developing relationship.

That was okay with Dillon. He could work with that type of prudence. He was willing to wait for Hunter's uncertainties to settle. And now that he'd witnessed Hunter's misgivings, he wondered if it was the same fear which had kept him awake the last few nights. Not that he couldn't undo all the things his family had done. But his unconscious worry that Hunter wouldn't want him for the rest of his life, that what he told Travis was just another wish that would never be granted. He felt an enormous and sudden relief flush through his body and he relaxed.

"So, how about some breakfast?" he asked.

Hunter was still chewing on his lip, but Dillon's question completely changed his demeanor. "I'm standing here butt-ass naked and you ask me that? Fuck breakfast. I want you, right now, right here," Hunter said and took Dillon's face in his hands again.

"You're not naked, you're still wearing socks," Dillon remarked with a smirk.

Hunter's mouth started to open with a retort, but he snapped it shut and reached down to strip his socks off. When he stood upright, he threw his hands out as if waiting for Dillon's next complaint.

"Jesus Christ, you're beautiful," Dillon murmured.

Hunter smiled and Dillon watched as a blush ran right up from his toes and colored his face. Hunter turned, felt for the breakfast bar, and bent over the counter, poking his ass into the air in anticipation.

Dillon rubbed his erection through his shorts as he stared at Hunter's body. Hunter was demanding the weight of his cock inside him. He wanted the heat of Dillon's core, the center of Dillon's lust filling him and making him feel the words Dillon had uttered this morning. Could he do that? Could he show Hunter how hard it had been to formulate those words, but how quickly they fell from his mouth when he looked at Hunter?

He unzipped his shorts and dropped them to the floor beside Hunter's boxers. His cock sprung up hard and jutted out in front of him with a thick heavy lust as he leered at Hunter's ass.

He ran his hand across the smooth, tight cheeks, up across Hunter's back, and then back down again. He slid his thumb across Hunter's hole and made him squirm and whimper as he pressed against the hot opening.

He smacked Hunter's ass. "Stay," he said before he went to the bedroom.

Dillon came back and stroked his cock, lubing each hard vein and the thick bulbous head. He swiped it up and down the crack of Hunter's ass, feeling the sweaty heat tingle and twitch against the sensitive tip as Hunter's sphincter flexed and groped at him.

'Mm," Hunter groaned. "Don't tease me, just fuck me. Fuck me hard."

Dillon ran his hand across Hunter's back again and grinned. "What's up with you lately?" He could feel Hunter's ass trying to clamp around the tip of his cock. Hunter was horny when he woke up. He just wanted to feel a hard, hot piece of man-meat in his ass. Dillon spread his cheeks wide and dribbled some lube over his sphincter. He ground his cockhead into Hunter's hole but didn't enter.

"Please," Hunter begged. He reached back to grab at Dillon's hips, but Dillon swatted his hands away.

Dillon lined his cock up and rammed it in until he felt his

nuts bump hot against Hunter's ass. Hunter went up on his toes, a breath exploding from between his teeth, his knuckles going white as he reached across and gripped the opposite side of the counter.

Hunter's breathing leveled out and he stood flat-footed again as his body got used to being filled. Dillon lifted him and watched as his body shivered under his ample breadth. He grabbed Hunter's ass in his hands and slammed his cock in again, raising Hunter from the floor. He separated Hunter's cheeks with his thumbs and began lifting his hips up and down against the motion of his thrusts. He pulled Hunter's ass down to the very base of his cock and slowly pulled him up until the ridge of his cockhead was just about to free itself.

Hunter was lost. His torso was pressed flat against the countertop, his fingers gripped its opposite side, and his cock was pushed down against the hardwood of the cabinets below. Dillon could see the moisture building up under his palms as he rammed into him over and over again.

"Yes," Hunter cried.

Dillon squeezed his thighs tighter and hoisted Hunter to his toes again, clasping his ass before bringing him down and slamming his cock deep into his guts. "Like that?" he demanded.

"Yes, more," Hunter gasped.

He grabbed Hunter by the hair and jerked him upright as he continued his assault. Slamming his cock in, he reached around and twisted Hunter's nipple. "Get down on the floor," Dillon growled in his ear.

"No." It was a petulant little denial, one that was weak and waiting to be overpowered.

Dillon snatched him further away from the counter, turned him, and bent him over so he had nothing to lean on. He tapped the back of Hunter's knee with his toe, bent it, and threw Hunter off-balance so he could push him to the floor.

Hunter winced as his knees hit the cold tile and then moaned as his palms slapped flat.

Dillon stood above him, his cock hard and red and standing out straight. He could see that Hunter loved the dominance in his actions. He had his ass pert and ready for more abuse, jutting into the air and waiting for him to fill it again. He knelt, gripped Hunter's muscled thighs and began slamming into him; thrusting in so hard and deep that Hunter was pushed across the floor and forced down to his elbows. He continued slamming into him.

"Turn over," Dillon demanded as he pulled his cock free.

"No," Hunter whimpered, his head hung down. "No."

Dillon shoved him on his side and grabbed his ankles, jerking them in the air as he rolled Hunter on his back against the cold floor. He pinned Hunter's legs against his shoulders, aimed at the hole he'd just left, and fell over him. He shoved his cock in and buried it to the hilt as he dove down to met Hunter's lips.

Hunter screamed against the quick, hard, rush of flesh. He opened his legs wider and shot his tongue into Dillon's mouth when their lips touched.

Dillon sneered and pulled his lips away as Hunter's mouth

yawned open. He watched Hunter roll his head back against the floor, the muscles of his neck protruding as the ache of wanton desire raced through him.

"You want this cum?" Dillon demanded, his sweat falling in hot wet drops against Hunter's torso. "Is that what you want?"

He could feel Hunter's ass clenching around his cock, goading him to cum. He didn't need a verbal reply. Hunter's whole body was begging for it; the ripe scent of his musk, the clasping of his guts, the fact that his toes were all stretched and spread as if grasping at the air. He steepled his hands across the top of Hunter's head and locked him in place as he battered Hunter's ass.

His hips became a fast, blurred motion as his cock slammed into Hunter. He continued to fuck him at that speed until Hunter was whimpering and trembling beneath him. He felt a thick, hot wetness between them and knew Hunter had cum. But he kept battering against him, his lust a hard, hot, angry rush that needed a release.

He could feel the surge building inside as Hunter moaned and thrashed. He pulled out and quickly rose to his knees as Hunter whimpered at the unexpected emptiness.

"No," Hunter gasped.

He grabbed Hunter by the neck and lifted him, stroking his cock as he brought Hunter's face up to meet its most secret pleasure. His cum sprayed across Hunter's lips, through his hair, and across the floor. They were hard, powerful jets that Hunter lapped at, his tongue flickering through the air until his hand came up and grabbed at Dillon's cock. He took it into his mouth and sucked on it with a hungry rumbling in his throat. He wanted it, wanted all that hot juice in his mouth.

Dillon arched back, another spurt racing out of him as he looked down at Hunter's ravenous mouth. He took Hunter's head in both hands and thrust deep into his throat as the final spurt wracked through his body.

"Oh fuck," he yelled. He came so hard he was shaking, twitching; the adrenaline coursing through his body had hardened every muscle as it pushed out the hot stink of sex. He pulled out and fell to the floor beside Hunter in a breathless, sweaty mess.

Hunter sat up and wiped his face with his forearm. "That was fucking hot." He grinned.

Dillon laughed and leaned over and kissed him. "What you do to me…" he shook his head unable to explain it. But after three days of no sex, Hunter's body did have that much of an effect on him. "Are you ready for breakfast now?" he asked as he pushed a stray hair from Hunter's face.

"I think so. Let me get cleaned up first."

Dillon watched him get up with a small wince as he ambled off to the bathroom. He wasn't surprised Hunter was sore; his own dick was still throbbing. He heard the shower start and got to his feet. He started a new pot of coffee, wiped himself down with a wet towel, and began to whistle. He suddenly had a better outlook on the coming day.

***

Hunter came back into the kitchen, dressed this time, and

gave Dillon another kiss before he went back to sit in front of the new cup of coffee Dillon had poured.

"Do you know what will be the best thing about you taking over the kitchen?" Hunter asked as Dillon turned the burner back on and pulled the sauté pan forward.

"The sex?" Dillon asked with a smirk.

Hunter laughed. "That shit's good, no matter what room we're in. No, I won't have to organize it anymore. You have no idea how much I loathe labeling food when I don't even like cooking."

"So…you'll be dependent on me?" Dillon pointed out with his question.

Hunter bristled. "Why do you have to be so logical? Now I have to go through and organize your kitchen. Shit."

"You're not going to blame me when you can't find a beer in the fridge," Dillon said, amused.

"Hmm, good point."

"Besides, I'll need help when we entertain, won't I?" Dillon asked.

"Entertain?" Hunter asked. "You mean people?"

Dillon laughed. "Yes, lover, people. Bipeds like us. They come around every once in a while for things like parties and holidays and…anniversaries."

"I've never done that."

"Because you can't cook worth a damn," Dillon teased.

"So you can cook and I'll entertain," Hunter suggested.

Dillon laughed. "You're going to stick me in the kitchen like some whipped puppy? I don't think so."

"Hmm," Hunter considered it. "Maybe just in your skivvies…"

Dillon still smelled like sex and he watched Hunter breathe it in like the aroma intoxicated him. Does he want to go again? he wondered.

"Or better yet," Hunter continued, "how about just an apron; one of those little French things with a G-string in the back? It will make those sightlings drool over what they can't have."

"Uh," Dillon feigned his indignation.

"We'd have the best-attended parties in Atlanta," Hunter countered.

Dillon laughed again. "I'm sure we would."

"Can I ask you something?" Hunter asked as he took another sip of his coffee.

"Sure."

"Have you ever... I mean with all the years…"

"What's your question?" Dillon asked as he tossed the ingredients into the pan. There was a minute of hot sizzle before Hunter finally brought up the courage to speak again.

"Have you ever had a boyfriend?"

He said it so quickly that Dillon had to look at him, a small laugh coming out as he noted how uncomfortable Hunter was about the question. "Sure," he answered.

"What happened?" Hunter asked.

"Nothing happened, that was the problem. They were…I

don't know. The relationships just never went anywhere. It was probably me more than anything."

"Because you were hustling?"

Dillon glanced at him again as he turned the flame down. "Oh, this is a serious conversation, huh?"

Hunter shrugged.

"There was another hustler one time," Dillon answered, "but he developed a drug problem and it was over pretty quick. I had a couple more here and there. One guy thought it was cool that I was a prostitute. Eventually, I realized that he just wanted to watch. Then...let's see, there was a yuppie conservative from Tennessee, but he had too many political dreams and finally decided he couldn't be associated with a male prostitute. I think he's married to some fish now. The last guy didn't like my kitchen. He was a real winner."

"Your kitchen?" Hunter asked.

"Yeah, can you believe it? It wasn't this kitchen. It was the one in my first apartment. I like to shop at the Asian market. Most of the stuff, you'll be labeling with Braille has Chinese labels. He hated that. He said they made him feel inferior because he couldn't read them."

Hunter chuckled. For some reason, it struck him as funny. "Was he?"

"Yes, that's why I did it," Dillon laughed. "He was an asshole who thought he was better than everyone else. But now I just buy the stuff because I like the market better than the big American stores."

Hunter laughed. "Cruel."

"Don't-cha-know?" Dillon quipped. "After him, I decided enough was enough and I let my friendship with Shawn sit in place of dating and relationships." He thought for a moment. "I guess I sort of folded in on myself."

Hunter was quiet.

"What about you?" Dillon asked.

"There were a couple of guys here and there," Hunter answered vaguely. "So why me?"

Dillon tilted his head and looked at Hunter curiously before he turned his gaze back to the stove. This was the real question. "Why not?" he asked Hunter. "You're a beautiful man with a big heart. You also have convictions that don't depend on you being the judge of other people."

"But you couldn't know that the first time," Hunter said.

Dillon struggled with the words as he tried to explain how Hunter had made him feel that first time. He poured the eggs into the pan. "It was the way you touched me. How you explored every single inch of me before you put your hands on me," Dillon admitted. "That first time we were in bed you searched out all the erogenous zones with your fingers, probably without even realizing it. It was subtle but very…tactile. It made me feel wanted, I mean more than just physically." He shrugged. He'd thought a lot about that night when he'd been beating himself up over bringing back Hunter's money. It wasn't the sex itself, but the how of it. Something he still couldn't explain to himself, let alone explain to

Hunter.

"I always felt like an experiment with other guys," Hunter blurted. "Like they were trying me out to see what it was like to fuck a blind man. It pissed me off."

Dillon paused, his hand hovering over the top of the pan. "Is that how you feel with me?" Now that he knew Hunter had been awake when he whispered I love you this morning, he was worried about what was running through Hunter's head. He hadn't wanted to voice those words out loud with any frequency until he thought Hunter was ready to fully accept them.

Hunter frowned. "Do you honestly think I'd be here if I felt like your experiment?"

"No." Dillon looked down at the omelet he created. He honestly didn't know what to think sometimes. Just when he thought he had a handle on reading Hunter, his insight disappeared and he was left guessing again. But maybe that was the part of a relationship he'd never discovered before – accepting his partner wholly rather than trying to speculate on what was coming next. "Breakfast is ready."

He grabbed a couple of plates and divided up the omelet, dropping toast down while Hunter got up and poured more coffee for both of them. When they sat down side by side Hunter grabbed his arm.

"Thanks," Hunter said quietly.

Dillon looked at him. This was an easy one for him to read. Hunter wasn't ready yet. That's what the thank you was for. For the space to feel his heart out and not feel pressured into doing so. "Sure," Dillon answered. "What time are you supposed to meet Margie?"

"Around two, but I need to stop by my apartment and go through a few recordings first."

"Coming back tonight?" Dillon asked.

"If you'll have me. I want to put a few hours in at the dojo too."

Dillon leaned into him with a kiss for an answer. "Eat before it gets cold," he added with a final peck on the tip of his nose.

Chapter 15

"Look, it's the Batman! We must be back on schedule," Connie announced when Hunter walked in the Rat Hole. He thought it was odd how quickly she cued into his mood when he walked in the door. He knew he couldn't hide his emotions well, but she was like his personal barometer.

He shrugged. "I couldn't be without you for any length of time, Connie."

"Shee-ut. That beautiful boy you got and you couldn't be without me?" She laughed at him. "You a straight fool, that boy is stupid over you. If you can't see it then you're not only blind, but dumb as hell too," Connie informed him.

He stopped on his way to the table and turned to her voice. "He likes you. I can't figure out why."

"All them pretty white boys love this big chocolate bunny," she cooed at him.

They burst out laughing together and he went to sit at his regular table.

"So, how was your Thanksgiving?" he asked Margie as he sat down. "Did you like your chocolate bunny too?"

She seemed to hold her breath before she answered. "It was different."

"Details, give me details."

"I met her family." Margie offered. "Her brothers are all as big as Connie and just as scary, but she runs them like a drill sergeant. It's actually funny. We had a nice time. I felt…welcome."

"No sex?" Hunter asked.

"Unlike you and your hot rod boyfriend, we're taking this a little slower, getting to know each other first."

"So she's not licking the plum yet, is that what you're trying to say?"

She gasped. "Hunter!"

He started laughing. "Oh, it's okay for you to ask if I got some ass, but not for me to ask you?"

"Do you have to be so crude?"

"Okay, I get it. You're still trying to figure out if you really want to go the bi route. That's cool." He laughed again. "What's up for today?"

"Saxby."

"Ugh, not today," Hunter moaned. He was in too good of a mood for Saxby. "Can we cancel?"

"No."

Connie interrupted with a coffee pot in hand. She put a cup down for Hunter and filled it. "The special?"

"Not today. I ate this morning."

"Oh, the pretty white boy making you breakfast already, huh?"

Hunter beamed.

"From the way you're stepping it looks like that cane wasn't the only thing swinging this morning either."

Hunter's smile froze on his face as she walked off with a laugh.

"She didn't," Hunter said.

Margie burst out laughing. "Yeah, she did. Come strutting in here like you own the world and you should expect it."

He smiled and leaned across the table towards her, lowering his voice. "You want to hear about it, don't you?"

"Not particularly. We've got work to do."

"OK, shoot," he replied, wanting all the tedious business affairs out of the way.

They worked three hours without taking a break until Connie finally suggested that they eat. Hunter ordered two specials. He hadn't realized just how much he'd let slip by while he was dealing with Dillon and made a mental note to keep better track of his business. Margie had gone easy on him at their last meeting because of all the drama in his life. But regardless of what was happening with Dillon, the bills still had to be paid and he still had contractual obligations that could put him at serious financial risk if he screwed up. By the fourth hour, they had worked through everything except Saxby, who came stomping up to the table with his usual heavy-footed odor of cheap cigars and stale human sweat.

They were twenty minutes into their conversation when Saxby suddenly stopped. "You seem different," Saxby informed him.

"What?" The comment threw Hunter completely off. They

were talking about renegotiating a contract if it did as well as Hunter expected it would. Saxby wanted more of the cut, which Hunter wasn't necessarily inclined to do. But Saxby had brought him two substantial winners in the last few months and throwing him a bone on this one author might keep the flow going and expand both their revenues.

"You get laid or something?" Saxby asked. "You seem more...relaxed."

"What the hell does that have to do with business?" Hunter asked.

"Nothing, it just makes it easier," Saxby answered. "You're not such an asshole."

Hunter heard Margie snickering from across the table. Just wait until her turn came around. "Thanks, can we get back to business now?"

***

"You never said how things went at your mom's house on Thanksgiving," Margie said after they finished with Saxby.

"It was kind of rough, for everyone. My mom was acting a little weird too. We talked about my dad."

"Your dad?"

"Yeah, like I said, it was weird."

"How did Dillon make out with his cousin?" Margie asked.

Hunter shrugged. Dillon hadn't spoken about it much and Hunter was quickly coming to understand that Dillon kept everything wrapped up inside until he was ready to burst. That wasn't healthy, but Hunter didn't want to push either.

"It was…strained. I still want to deck Travis," he told Margie.

"Not your place."

"Yeah, I know. But that doesn't change how I feel." He shrugged. "So I have this hypothetical question for you…"

"Good lord, just spit it out," Margie said after she waited for him to continue.

He hesitated. "I'm thinking about moving in with Dillon."

"You are?"

"I know it's too soon and all the other rational excuses that make it complete nonsense, but I think I want to. You know, something more…permanent."

She laughed. "Isn't that this same drama we went through last month? Oh no, I'm wrong. Last month you were worried about calling it a relationship, wasn't that it?"

He sneered at her in reply and drank his coffee.

"Have you talked to Dillon?" Margie asked.

"He already asked me to move into his place," Hunter answered.

"So why the hell are you asking me? You don't need my permission."

"I didn't ask," Hunter informed her. "I'm talking to you because you're supposed to be the person giving me all the reasons it's such a stupid idea."

"Will this impact your work?" she asked.

"Work isn't a sticking point. I'm just changing locations so it shouldn't have a significant effect on anything. I may be down for a couple of days, but not much else."

"So what is the sticking point?" She didn't understand the purpose of the conversation.

"He said he loved me this morning," Hunter told her, "for the second time."

"More drama," Margie intoned with a voice that said he was quickly wearing out her patience. "Thanks for inviting me in. Why is this a problem?"

"That's a big fucking jump, don't you think? From let's move in together to I love you. I don't even know what to say to that."

"Usually you say something like I love you too, but it sounds like you're making excuses to me."

"You're supposed to be on my side," Hunter argued.

"Oh no," she informed him. "You're not putting me on anyone's side. There is no side. Move in; don't move in. It doesn't mean shit to me either way. I'm staying out of this."

"You've never stayed out of it before."

"You've never run around like a star-struck moron before either. We've talked about the sex end of things with your other men because it was nothing serious, just a quick fuck. This is entirely different. This is you getting involved."

"So you don't have my back anymore?"

"Why is it that every effing homo I know is great at business, but a damned grade-schooler when it comes to a relationship?" she asked. "I don't need to have your back. You already made the decision to move in. Now you're just looking for excuses to not go through with it."

"It's not that," Hunter argued. "I haven't told him I'm moving in yet. I mean I have but... I just don't know if I'm in love with him. What if...I don't know...What if I don't love him and all this is just another fling?"

"Bitch, please. You're turning this into another dilemma, which isn't the Hunter I know. Has he got you that scared?"

Hunter turned his mouth down at her comment. "Okay, okay, whatever. I'm just asking for your perspective. If you don't want to give it, fine."

"My perspective?" Margie asked.

"Yeah."

"Here's my perspective. You've been fucking like rabbits since you met and crooning over each other like a couple of seventh-grade sweethearts. Hell, you're probably already having unsafe sex but I know you wouldn't dare tell me because you know I'd rip your head off. How am I doing so far?"

Hunter said nothing.

"Thought so. Idiot."

"We're both clean," Hunter said in defense.

"Really? How do you know?" Margie demanded. "He's a fucking prostitute."

"Was."

"Was, is. It doesn't make a difference now, does it? If he's infected, then so are you. How do you think your mom would take it?"

"Margie," Hunter warned.

"Oh, too close to home? Wouldn't want your mom watching you disintegrate on her couch? You know about my brother. You know what I went through with him."

"Your brother was a junkie, Margie. This is different."

"He fucking died of AIDS," she spat, banging her fist on the table. "And I had to watch him do it."

"Margie, I'm sorry, that's not what I meant," Hunter stammered. He knew her story. It had happened a few years before they met, but it had been one of the few personal things she'd shared with him about her family. Her parents had written her brother off completely because of it and she hadn't seen or spoken to them since he died. "It just happened," he explained.

She scoffed at him. "And kept happening? What excuse are you going to give me next, that men can't think when their dick gets hard? Have you two even talked about getting tested?" she questioned.

Again Hunter was silent.

"See. So here you come asking me my opinion about shit that doesn't matter and neither of you have even given a single second of consideration about something that does. Pretty fucking pathetic, don't you think?"

"Sorry I even asked."

"You should be, and if you really want to turn this into more than whatever you think you have, then you should've been thinking about these things without me getting on your ass."

He sighed. "You're right. I'll talk to him today. But…the rest of it?"

"What kind of answer are you looking for, Hunter? You're a grown man. If you feel that strongly about him, then go for it. If not…Well, you're going to have to break it to him, and soon."

"I do feel it. I'm just not sure how deep yet."

He could almost hear her rolling her eyes before she even spoke. "Whatever. You make it sound like you're trying to decide what to order in this shit-hole restaurant," she dismissed his misgivings. "You'll see it, or you'll blow it. Or is it the word you're afraid of?" she asked him. She leaned in close, watching his body movements as he turned away from the sound of her voice. "That's it, isn't it? You didn't have a problem with any of it until you actually heard him say the word love."

"I..." He closed his mouth and reached for his coffee. She was right, and now that she said it aloud it made the point obvious, and pathetic. How many times in his life had he wished to hear those words? Hadn't he already told his mother he loved Dillon? And now, when the words were spoken aloud and his heart was definitely filled with the same feeling he was stumbling. Pathetic.

"Typical fag," Margie said. "Run down to your dojo acting all macho, go home and spread your legs when the wind blows, but you're shit-scared to open up because you're worried about…what?

That you might get hurt? It's part of the territory, Hunter. It's a give and take."

"Thanks for being so helpful."

"You want me to blow smoke up your ass? Have I ever done that?"

"No," he answered quietly. Margie had never done that. It was one of the reasons he trusted her as both a friend and a business partner. She could be crass, but she'd never misled him or allowed him to delude himself with indulgent fantasies.

"No," she repeated. "So now you figure I'm going to start doing it because…" She waited for him to finish for her.

He backed down. "You're right. Okay? You're right. Is that what you want to hear? I was in bed for an hour wondering how I was supposed to answer him. I didn't know what to say. I still don't."

"So you just fucked instead?"

"Yeah," he admitted.

"Men," Margie exasperated as she shook her head. "You really want to know why you're having such a problem?" she asked.

He nodded.

"Because you're a control freak just like your mom, that's why," she informed him. "Everything you do, the martial arts, the business, your obstinacy when it comes to being independent is all about Hunter being in control. But ever since you met Dillon, you've been out of control, and you can't hang."

"You think I'm a control freak?" Hunter asked.

"I don't think it, I know it. Look how you took the news of your mom. You wouldn't even think of taking her out of the box you stuck her in until I got on your ass. That's control. She has to be what you think she should be. Sweet little mom baking apple pies for you when you decide to go home, instead of a grown ass woman who likes a good, raw fuck like any other human being."

"I'm not like that," Hunter sputtered. He hadn't expected this type of assault, not even from Margie.

"Aren't you? You get all pissy when things don't go your way. You always have. And now Dillon's got you completely fucked up because you aren't in control of your own emotions," Margie informed him. "Sounds to me like you're trying to put him in another box; one that only opens when Hunter is ready. It won't work and it won't last if that's what all this bullshit is really about."

"Fuck," Hunter murmured "Anything else?"

She smirked. "Got any more stupid questions you want me to answer?"

"No, none," Hunter replied instantly.

"Good, now stop acting like a goddamned drama queen. It's getting on my nerves."

"Is that really what you think about me? That I'm a control freak?" He was hurt by her words, but he also found some truth in them and realized maybe it was why they bothered him so much.

"Yes," she answered. "Control has a time and place, Hunter, and you won't always have it. It's just something you're going to have to learn and accept. If you really love Dillon, then you'd be goddamned stupid to let him go because you're afraid of the word. Or what you think the word entails."

"I'm not afraid," he reiterated. "Besides, I thought you didn't like him."

She scoffed at him and remained silent.

Chapter 16

Time seemed to be moving faster. They were almost halfway through December and had begun to settle into a routine. Hunter worked all day at his apartment, went about regular business with Margie, and kept up his practice at the dojo. Then he'd settle in for the night at his own place, or more and more often, at Dillon's. The invitation to move in with Dillon was still open, but he hadn't made a decision yet.

Today, they'd planned a quiet day together away from all business and friends. It was one of those rare midweek days when Hunter didn't have anything pressing. And even though Dillon didn't know it, Margie had strongly suggested Hunter spend some time with Dillon and make a fucking decision so they could get back to normal.

"I thought we could just have a simple dinner — roasted chicken, a quick salad, and some fresh bread. How's that sound?" Dillon asked.

"No microwave? How will I know if all the germs have been killed?"

"You may just have to suffer without the knowledge."

"As I curl up in gastrointestinal anguish…" Hunter teased.

Dillon smiled. Hunter seemed to be warming to the idea of food cooked without a microwave. But what he seemed to enjoy more, was that Dillon not only had a knack for cooking, but had begun to experiment and try to broaden his culinary knowledge.

Last week, he spoke to Hunter about attending culinary school, but it seemed less and less attractive as he explored the idea. He didn't want to be a professional chef and he certainly didn't relish spending fifteen hours a day in a kitchen away from Hunter.

There was a knock on the front door and Hunter turned his face to the sound. "Are you expecting someone?"

"No," Dillon glanced at him briefly and shifted his gaze to the door. "And even if I were, they'd have to check in at the security desk and call up first. You're the only person who has clearance to come in. That's why we gave them all your information." He didn't tell Hunter that he'd listed him as another occupant on the forms they filled out, and not as a regular, long-term guest as Hunter supposed. As far as anyone in the building knew, Hunter was already a resident.

"I like the sound of that," Hunter said. He put his hand out and let his fingers drag across Dillon's thigh as he passed.

"Be careful," Dillon warned, turning back to him with a small peck on his cheek. "You're going to get me all hot and sweaty before we eat."

"Hmm, well maybe you can interrogate me and see if my clearance is valid," Hunter suggested.

Dillon laughed as a second, more insistent knock came. "Must be one of the neighbors," he said as he pulled away from Hunter and went to the door. But the neighbors in his building didn't knock on doors to chit-chat. It wasn't that type of complex. In all the time he'd live there, he'd only seen his neighbors twice and only in passing.

When he opened the door and saw his mother, Abigail, he could only stare. Shock hit him first, then outrage. Travis was standing behind her.

Dillon's breath choked in an instant fury. Hunter came to stand behind him, no doubt alerted by his sudden inhalation.

"What the fuck are you doing here?" Dillon demanded.

Abigail had aged – her face had a few more wrinkles, her dark hair had more wisps of gray than black, but it was her eyes that hadn't changed. They still held the same sharp revulsion that they did when she'd slammed the door behind him ten years prior.

"I want you to come home. You're living in sin," Abigail said.

"I'm not going anywhere with you," Dillon spat.

"Pastor Harvey said I needed to confront you and bring you home. I admit I was wrong for throwing you out, but your father…"

"Don't you dare say another word about my father," Dillon growled. There wasn't even a hint of an apology in her voice, just a conviction that she'd failed in her religious duty. It only added to his rage. A quick image of his father's gravestone flickered through his mind. He could feel the cords of his neck stand out as he remembered how desolate he'd felt looking at the single inscription. It was as if he'd been completely negated from his father's life, from any life at all.

"Pastor Harvey…" she began again.

"Pastor Harvey can go fuck himself."

Hunter squeezed his shoulder in reassurance as his hands clenched into fists. He didn't doubt Hunter wanted to slap her as much as he did. He breathed and patted Hunter's hand, watching his mother's eyes dart to Hunter's face and the hand he put on Dillon's shoulder.

"Dillon, you need to come home and get right with God." She scowled when she looked at him again. "And I need you back. I'm by myself now." She reached out to put her hand on his arm to emphasize her point.

Dillon gaped at her. He was completely at a loss at her audacity to suggest such a thing and jerked his arm from her grasp. He was only at eye level when he was sixteen, but now at twenty-six he towered over her, all his anger and hurt pushing through every single muscle in his body. She used to remind him of the brilliance of his eyes and how he'd inherited them from his father, the trait which had made her notice his dad the first time they met. Now those same eyes were staring back at her with utter rage. "Maybe you should've thought of that before you threw me into the street," he fumed, the muscles of his jaw tight with fury.

Hunter silently caressed his arm again and he felt a small portion of his ire drain away. He took a deep breath to calm himself. Hunter had given him something to look forward to again. He wouldn't allow this bitch to contaminate what they'd started building together.

"You're right," she conceded. But her words and her bearing were as mocking as her stiff posture. "That was a poor way to handle the situation. We could've gotten you therapy or something."

"Fuck you and your therapy," Dillon snapped. "Why did you bring her here?" he barked at Travis, who stood silently behind her. He turned back to his mother. "Don't ever come near me again. We have nothing to say to each other."

"Sodomites burn in hell," she barked with a disgusted snort.

He leaned down and put his face in hers. "I guess I'll see you there, because you damned sure aren't Christian. Now get the fuck out of my house."

Travis took a step forward. "Dillon…"

"And you can get the fuck out too," Dillon barked at him. "Both of you."

"I just wanted to give you two a chance," Travis argued.

"Well, you gave it to me. It's done. You're off the hook. Thanks for nothing. Now get the fuck out."

"Just remember this," Abigail ranted. "It wasn't me that burned your stupid boat. It was your father. You think he wasn't disgusted? He despised what you'd become and you broke his heart. He died praying for your soul. You killed him." She leveled her finger at him to emphasize the point. Dillon lunged. His mind was a white hot rage.

Hunter's arms locked around him instantly and snatched him back. He pinned Dillon against his chest as Dillon struggled and flayed to get to her. He gritted his teeth in a tight rage but stopped fighting after a moment. Hunter didn't let him go.

"Get the fuck out of here," he seethed. "I'll kill you if I see you again. I swear it, I'll kill you."

"Dillon," Hunter whispered into his ear as he held him. "Shh. It's a lie. What she just said is a lie. I can hear it in her voice. I love you. Don't let her get into your head. It's a lie. I promise you."

Her eyes narrowed as she glared at Hunter. Her visible animus toward Hunter only enraged Dillon more. Let her threaten Hunter and he'd tear her to pieces and dump the parts down the elevator shaft.

"It's God's honest truth!" she barked.

"No, it's not," Travis stated from behind her.

Abigail's breath caught and she whirled on him. Dillon became still and stared at them in utter disbelief. What the fuck was going on?

Travis hung his head and blew out a long breath before he spoke. "Your father called me before he died, Dillon. He wanted you back home. He wanted you to know he loved you. He didn't hate you, Dillon. He never did. He just didn't know how to handle your sexuality. That's the truth."

"That's a lie!" Abigail yelled.

"No, it's not," Travis reiterated quietly. "He knew you weren't going to get in touch with Dillon before he died. He asked you, but he knew you wouldn't, and now Dillon knows it too."

He lifted his head. "I'm sorry, Dillon. I should've told you sooner, but I thought...I didn't..." He shrugged in complete defeat and dropped his head again. "I guess it doesn't matter what I thought. I'm sorry, for everything." He turned and walked back to the elevator, leaving Abigail standing in the doorway.

Dillon deflated in Hunter's arms; his rage completely shattered. He had tears clinging to his lashes at Travis' words, but he wouldn't let them fall, not in front of her.

"You're disgusting," he spat as his mother turned to face him again. He saw her arrogance was gone, but not her loathing. "Don't ever come back here again or I'll have you arrested," he told her as he shrugged Hunter's arms off.

She looked at him for a second, glanced at Hunter and turned on her heel, her mouth a moue of contempt and disgust. "Then burn in hell, sodomites."

Dillon slammed the door and fell back on it. His stomach was in knots. Before he knew it, Hunter was lifting him into his arms as he began to slide to the floor. "This can't be happening…" His breath came out in an anguished sob.

Hunter was talking to him, he heard the words, saw his mouth move, but they didn't register. Travis hadn't called. His father had died wanting to see him and no one had called…

He stared at Hunter, his eyes watering. He was trembling and trying to hold ten year's worth of animosity in once again. Just a few short weeks ago they were in the same predicament at Hunter's apartment. Would he ever be free of these people? Would he ever be free of their hold on his life?

He took a deep breath and stood upright. He wouldn't fall

apart like last time. "I…I'm sorry. Just give me a minute. I'll be okay."

As Hunter backed off, Dillon looked at his face and saw the coiled rage. He was irate but desperately trying to let it go and just be there. It gave Dillon the boost of support he needed and bolstered his own strength. He could not change what was done, but he could make sure his family never interfered in his life again. "I need to call downstairs," he mumbled.

He walked around Hunter, not quite ready for another embrace, and snatched up the phone. He left specific instructions at the security desk that neither Abigail nor Travis was ever to be allowed into the building again and then demanded to know how they had gotten up to his apartment in the first place. He listened and wanted to scream at the guard for being so goddamned stupid, but he put the phone down and turned back to Hunter instead.

Hunter hadn't moved. He was still standing by the door, his body full of tension and ready to spring at a moment's notice. Just like the night the mugger came after them.

"Sorry…I… The security desk said my mother claimed it was my birthday and wanted to surprise me," Dillon told him.

"And they bought it?" Hunter asked.

"Apparently." He took another deep breath as he tried to calm himself. "Sorry," he said again.

Hunter was in front of him in a second. It amazed him at how fast Hunter could move sometimes. He reached down and took Dillon's hands. "Stop saying that. You handled it better than I would have. You have nothing to be sorry about."

He squeezed back on Hunter's hands, the emotion right on the edge of his voice. "Were you ready to stomp them?" he asked, forcing humor into his voice. He needed this to be right between them. No, that wasn't it. He needed it to be gone and not be anything between them at all.

"Of course," Hunter answered. "Didn't you see me getting ready to do my secret flying ninja move? I would've taken them both out with my cane before I even landed; just flipped over your head and whap-whap, out cold."

"And shut and locked the door?" Dillon asked with a small smile. Even in his anger, Hunter's compassion was never completely wiped away.

"And shut and locked the door," Hunter affirmed. "And called security too."

Dillon kissed him lightly, the curve of his smile a little harder on his lips. "Those secret ninja tricks are amazing," he whispered as he touched Hunter's forehead with his own.

"Just wait until you see me do it naked."

Dillon laughed, cupped his head in his hands and kissed Hunter's lips. "Thanks."

Hunter shrugged, but Dillon could still see the anger knotted up inside. It had probably taken every fiber of Hunter's self-control not to physically toss them both into the elevator. He certainly would've ended up in prison had Hunter not been there to hold him back.

He grabbed Hunter's hand and led him back to the kitchen. He was determined not to let this ruin their day. "Come on. Let's finish what we were doing."

"Does that mean you're going to get naked?" Hunter asked as he allowed Dillon to drag him along.

"Naked?" Dillon stopped and turned back to him with a smirk. "We were organizing the kitchen...Well, you were. I was about to make dinner."

"Oh," Hunter said as he rubbed the bottom of his chin. "I thought you mentioned something about being naked and roasted something-or-other." He shrugged. "But I guess we can reorganize the kitchen instead."

Dillon chuckled and pulled him into his arms. "Naked and roasted, huh? Are you sure I wasn't talking about the chicken?"

Hunter nodded vigorously. A goofy grin lit his face as he wrapped his arms around Dillon's waist. He reached forward with a kiss which drew the anger from Dillon and developed into something more passionate.

"Well, maybe we should change the menu tonight," Dillon managed after sighing away from Hunter's lips.

"Now you're talking."

"How about mole de pavo, desnudo style?" Dillon asked.

Hunter's eagerness seemed to fall from his face in an instant and it made Dillon laughed.

"What the hell is that?" Hunter asked.

"Poor thing," he said as he pecked Hunter's lips. "Obviously not what you were talking about, it's a naked turkey breast cooked with poblano sauce."

Hunter's mouth folded into an exaggerated pout. It made Dillon snicker. "Not what you were thinking?" he asked.

"No," Hunter answered petulantly.

"Oh good, I don't have any of that stuff in the house. You have any suggestions?"

"I…could think of a few," Hunter offered eagerly.

He reached up and caressed Hunter's temple, pushing back the hair as he stroked around his ear. He saw Hunter's aim behind the amorous suggestions, but he doubted he could give Hunter the attention he deserved. "Can I take a rain check?" he asked quietly.

Hunter kissed him lightly. "Sure, but do I get the option to call it in whenever the mood strikes?"

"That might be an hour from now," Dillon teased.

"Or a minute," Hunter said as he wiggled his eyebrows. "What can I say? You're an excellent lover."

Dillon pulled him into a hard embrace and held him tight. "You're not so bad yourself, you know?"

"Hell, I know that. I'm the gay Don Juan of blind men," Hunter said with a swagger.

Dillon burst out laughing and let him go, giving him another kiss before he began pulling him back toward the kitchen. "Come on, we've got work to do, stud."

"Can I ask you something?" Hunter asked as they came into

the kitchen. He leaned up against the counter.

Dillon instantly recognized that while Hunter was trying to keep things light, he wasn't about to let Abigail's visit go so quickly. Nor was he going to let Dillon force the situation back down inside of himself like he usually did. "Sure," he answered.

"Do you think things with your mother could be fixed?" Hunter asked. "I mean if she had a change of heart?"

Dillon was quiet for a minute before he answered. "I don't think she'll ever change but…" He paused to collect his thoughts and started again. "Part of me wants to say yes because she's my mother, and then the other part of me rejects the idea altogether. Knowing what she did when I was most vulnerable, and knowing she probably already understood what I was about to face even when I didn't…" He shook his head. "But now that I know she kept me from my dad on purpose… No, it will never be fixed. I'll never forgive her." He was quiet again. "Are you okay with that?"

"Yes, completely," Hunter replied. "But I want to be sure you are."

Dillon looked at the city through the window behind Hunter as he spoke. "I think I always knew it was her. I mean…my dad was the one who always encouraged me to do the things I wanted to go for. He was always the motivator while she was always the naysayer, even when we built the boat. Did you hear her? She's still pissed about it ten years later. We named the fucking thing after her."

He didn't give Hunter a chance to respond but fell into another short but contemplative silence before he spoke again. "I think she was jealous. She acted like I was stealing her husband from her or something. I don't know how to explain it otherwise. No matter how much I've thought about it over the years nothing about that day makes any sense. My father was never like that, never." He sighed. "Can we just forget about this?"

Hunter came to him and touched his face. He traced his finger down Dillon's jawline. "You'll never forget it, Dillon. Not like that."

"I'm just not used to talking about my family," Dillon said as he lowered his eyes to the floor. He wanted this gone so desperately. He wanted things right between him and Hunter so they could go forward without his baggage dragging them down. That had been the point of their weekend together and the only reason he'd agreed to meet Travis over Thanksgiving. And then that fuck had brought her here. Now he had the truth about his father and…it made him feel worse. He hadn't thought that was possible.

He looked up at Hunter. Here was the reason he knew the truth. Hunter had stepped forward when he'd been too afraid and then stood beside him when the truth tumbled down on him like a pile of bricks. He reached out and caressed Hunter's cheek.

"Fair enough," Hunter said as Dillon touched him. He turned his face into Dillon's hand. "I just want you to know I'm here when you're ready. Okay?"

"Okay," he mumbled, still lost in thought. His mind drifted and he suddenly focused on Hunter's lips as he recalled his words. Hunter had been whispering in his ear as he raged at his mother.

"You said…you loved me?"

Hunter nodded quietly, his face flushing.

"But a few days ago…"

Hunter came into his arms before he could finish. "It's not that I don't love you, Dillon, I do. I'm…" He stopped and cleared his throat. "I'm afraid I can't love you enough. With everything you've been through…I…"

"You what?" Dillon asked. He needed these words, needed Hunter, but he needed Hunter to need him too. Did Hunter think he wasn't good enough? Did he think Dillon was too wounded to invest in? Love only went so far sometimes. Sometimes you had to cut it off to survive. Dillon knew that too well.

"I don't know if I'm man enough…" Hunter admitted as he blew out a breath in frustration. "I don't know if what I can offer you is enough. I know it sounds stupid, but…"

Dillon grabbed the sides of his face, his lips hot and insistent against the warmth of Hunter's kiss. He'd been obsessing over his own shortcomings since he met Hunter. How could Hunter think such a thing? "You are so much more than you understand, Hunter. You're more than enough. I've been afraid I'd taint you."

Hunter stuttered in surprise. "That's…ludicrousness. Taint me? I'm a thirty-year-old, blind fag who has hated the world for most of his adult life. How do you possibly think you can taint me?"

Dillon kissed him again, tentatively at first, then with a growing need. "I love you, Hunter. I do," he said with a deep breath as he pulled back. "From the second I saw you I just…I don't know,

I just knew."

"So…How about that roasted, spicy, sex thing we were talking about then?" Hunter asked with a smirk.

Dillon smiled as Hunter switched gears again. "Is that really what you want?" He started tugging him toward the bedroom. "Come on, I can see you're not going to give up."

Hunter held his ground and pulled Dillon back to him. Dillon noted that he'd lost his coquettish grin.

"What I want is for you to be happy with me. That's what I want," Hunter said.

"I am," Dillon answered quietly, not comprehending why Hunter didn't understand that already.

Hunter paused for a moment before he spoke again. "I think you might be happier if…"

"If what?" Dillon interrupted quickly. He didn't want to hear Hunter say something about being happier with someone else. It would kill him.

"If I moved in," Hunter finished. "Say…around Christmas?"

Dillon beamed. "You mean it? That's two weeks away."

Hunter nodded. "We've got some logistics to work out, but your mom's visit made me realize something."

"What?"

"That I really do love you, and that I'm not willing to let you go. I've been trying to stand back and let you make your own decision about your family but…fuck…I'm going to fight to keep you if I have to, Dillon. I'm not going to let you go back to that, to her. No way."

"My little ninja," Dillon whispered as he curled into Hunter's embrace.

Hunter grabbed at his crotch through his jeans and shook. "Ain't nothing little about this ninja," he cracked as Dillon began to laugh.

Chapter 17

"Why are we here exactly?" Hunter asked again as they pulled up in front of Shu-shu's store. Dillon had proposed the idea of going to meet Shu-shu after breakfast, and Hunter had agreed without even thinking. But now he felt apprehensive. He didn't understand it.

"You've met my family..." Dillon stopped talking for a moment. "Let me rephrase that. You've met the people who were supposed to be my family, and now I want you to meet the person who felt more like a parent to me than my own parents did."

"Shu-shu?" Hunter asked.

"Yes." He glanced over at him. "You seem nervous."

"I am," Hunter admitted. "Weren't you when we went to meet my mom?"

"I probably would've been, if I weren't so worried about making an ass of myself," Dillon chuckled.

"Yeah, well... How do you plan on introducing me?"

Dillon's brow furrowed. "As my boyfriend?" he offered tentatively.

"See, that's a first for me."

Dillon smiled quietly. "That's what you're worried about?"

Hunter shrugged.

"That's so cute," Dillon giggled before he leaned over the seat and kissed him on the cheek.

Hunter turned to him slightly, color rising in his face. "Cute? Thanks, now I actually feel stupid."

"He won't bite you, I promise."

"All right, come on." Hunter opened the car door and stepped out. "He just better be ready for my secret ninja tricks. That's all I'm saying," Hunter grinned as Dillon came around and took his arm.

"I'll make sure I warn him."

When they walked into the store, Hunter was instantly surrounded by an exotic bouquet of smells and odors which were unfamiliar to him. He loved it. Incense was wafting from somewhere on his right and a bounty of what smelled like dried herbs came from his left. He didn't smell any dried fish or durian, which usually made Chinese stores offensive to those unfamiliar with the sweet taste of the fruit's flesh. A grin lit his face at once.

He tugged on Dillon's arm and made him stop before they went into the back of the store. "Do they have a shrine?"

"A shrine?" Dillon repeated.

"Yes," Hunter insisted. He knew the question had undoubtedly drawn an odd look, but he had his reasons.

"Yes, there's a shrine in the back corner."

"Can you bring me to it?" Hunter asked.

Dillon led him to the back of the store and watched as Hunter placed his palms together and bowed to the shrine.

"Is there incense?" Hunter asked. He already knew the answer, but he wanted Dillon to guide his hand so he wouldn't upset anything.

"Yes," Dillon replied with curiosity in his voice.

Dillon took his hand and placed it on the table, guiding it to the joss sticks. He watched as Hunter took one, felt for something to light it with, and then measured it with his hand before he lit the end of it. He blew the flame out after a moment and took it between his palms and did three more bows. When he finished, he put his hand out for Dillon again and put the stick in the sand-filled receptacle.

"Okay. Let's meet Shu-shu."

"What was that about?" Dillon asked.

"Paying respects," Hunter told him.

"How did you know?" Dillon asked.

Hunter smiled. "Secret ninja instincts."

Dillon shook his head and led him back through the aisles to the back of the store. "Shu-shu?" he called out when they passed through the doorway.

The upstairs door banged open and Shu-shu's wife came flying down the stairs, her voice a loud babble of noise and tears. She stood in front of Hunter pleading in a language he couldn't understand as Dillon stared at her in shock.

"Dillon?" Hunter asked cautiously. "She's upset about something."

"She's going too fast," Dillon answered. "Something about wanting you to…read her?"

Hunter heard his confusion. Dillon had expounded on her previous animosity towards him and explained that because she was from a different province in China her dialect was different. Dillon had a hard time understanding her and thought it was just another one of the reasons she'd disliked him so steadfastly.

"Something about Bao…," Dillon said.

Shu-shu came in from the back dock, took one look at his wife, and barked an order in Chinese. They went back and forth for a few minutes before she went silent, her tears still punctuated by small sobs. Even though Hunter didn't understand a word of what was said, it took him only a moment to recognize that they'd had this particular argument many times before. Dillon translated as Shu-shu spoke.

"She says you're the master she was told would come. She wants you to read her and tell her news of Bao."

"What?" Hunter asked.

"Bao, their son, I told you about him. I think you just paid reverence at his shrine."

"Was there a picture?" Hunter asked.

"Yes."

Hunter sighed. He'd asked about the shrine and paid respects because he thought it might make a better impression than Dillon popping up with his queer lover in tow. Despite what Dillon said about Shu-shu's acceptance, he still had reservations. Having a dead gay brother wasn't the same as having two queers pawing at each other in front of you. "Ask Shu-shu what she's talking about. I don't understand."

Dillon spoke in Chinese and both Shu-shu and his wife started talking again. They went silent when Hunter held up his hand. This was getting nowhere. "What kind of master does she think I am?" He waited for Dillon to translate.

"Mien Shiang, face reading," Dillon explained as Shu-shu spoke. "He says his wife is convinced, and if you don't read her she'll die. She's been waiting for you since Bao's death."

Hunter swiveled his head in Dillon's direction in complete disbelief. "What the hell am I supposed to say?"

Dillon was silent. He was just as surprised as Hunter. "I…" He shook his head. "I don't know. She wants you to read her face."

"Isn't that a visual art; something about personality characteristics?" Hunter asked. He vaguely remembered reading about it online, but nothing specifically came to mind.

Dillon repeated his question and got an instant reply from Shu-shu. "That is a Western understanding clouded by Western thought. You are a master; vision is a veil which hides the truth of things," Dillon translated.

"What does that mean?" Hunter asked.

"That's what he said," Dillon shrugged.

Hunter answered with a small nod. Dillon was just as clueless as he was. But he didn't need sight to know the depth of this woman's sorrow. Her whole body gave off an aroma of despair so deep that it seemed to emanate right from her bones. He didn't know the art they spoke of, or what he was supposed to tell her, but if it helped her with the death of her son he wouldn't refuse either. What was a little fake hocus pocus if he could spare her some grief?

He reached out to her with his free hand, drawing his fingers across her face, feeling the salty grit of the tears still leaking down and the sorrow burned into her brow. He cupped her chin and felt along the sides of her jaw and... He didn't know what to say.

Suddenly he recalled a question from his earliest childhood. He was sitting in an old woman's lap which he now recognized as his father's mother. He was four, maybe five, and they were curled up together in a big chair in her house listening to morning cartoons. He remembered her discussing a photo and he'd asked why his father had died. He'd listened as her voice choked. Her answer had been simple and he shared it with Shu-shu and his wife.

"He went to prepare the path for you. You must not weep. It was his duty as a son, which he honored and which you must honor." He changed his grandmother's words considerably and placed them in the context of their beliefs. He could only hope that this was the kind of answer she was looking for.

Complete silence engulfed them until the woman barked at Dillon to translate what Hunter said. She burst into tears once she heard his words and fell into Hunter's arms weeping like a child until Shu-shu pulled her off and took her into his own embrace.

They both bowed to Hunter and then Shu-shu led her upstairs to their apartment. He gestured at them, indicating they should wait for his return. They listened to the muffled sobs trail off as the door closed.

"That was interesting," Hunter said with some relief. He didn't like being accosted in any manner, but having a grief-stricken woman demand answers he didn't have would probably top the list of improbabilities he thought he'd ever experience. Although, the more he thought about it, the more he realized how many uncertainties seemed to have occurred since he'd met Dillon.

"Where the hell did you come up with that answer?" Dillon asked.

Hunter shrugged. "Something my grandmother said when I asked why my father died."

"Sorry," Dillon said. "I didn't know anything about this. I honestly thought she was screaming at me for bringing you here until she mentioned Bao."

"Don't worry about it," Hunter replied, shrugging it off. "Maybe it will help."

"But why would she think that about you?" He paused, thinking. "They have cameras for the store upstairs. She must have seen you at the shrine."

"Could be," Hunter muttered.

"Weird."

"Yeah," Hunter agreed. But his mind was still recalling the tactile memories of his grandmother's embrace – the rose scented perfume she wore, and how she'd sit for hours and let him explore her face when he wanted to. She was the only person in his life that had ever allowed him to do that, and he was ashamed he'd forgotten. He made a mental note to ask his mother about his grandparents the next time he went home.

The door to the upstairs apartment opened again and Shu-shu called out to them instead of coming back down.

"He wants us to come up," Dillon said in surprise.

"I thought you said you'd never been invited upstairs before."

"I haven't. You must have said the right thing."

Hunter's brow folded. This was just a little too convenient. Blind Master shows up, throws down some ancient wisdom, and the world is suddenly all hunky-dory. He wasn't buying it.

The apartment was a clutter of boxes, foreign smells, and a woman who had quickly put aside her grief and intended to offer Hunter her thanks in any way she could find. Apparently that meant food, and lots of it.

Shu-shu led them into a small dining area while his wife buzzed around them chattering. In just a few moments, a pot of tea was set on the table and Shu-shu was pouring as if it were an official ceremony. He and his wife went back and forth in Chinese for a few moments and Dillon told him that Shu-shu was telling her that the tea was enough. She didn't have to cook too.

"I could eat," Hunter said.

Dillon translated and the woman turned and beamed at him. She scowled at her husband and turned back to what she was doing. Dillon chuckled and told him what had happened.

Shu-shu spoke again and Dillon translated. "Shu-shu says thank you. You seem to have given him back his wife."

"Is that a good thing?" Hunter asked.

Dillon translated and Shu-shu boomed with laughter. "We'll see."

"He also just gave me a nod of approval about you," Dillon said with a smile in his voice.

"Ah, didn't know I was on the block," Hunter smirked. "Now I know how you felt meeting my mom."

"Your mom was easy. Margie was hell."

Hunter nodded in agreement and listened to them go back and forth. "Shu-shu speaks English," he announced. He'd listened to the different inflections of their speech and compared it with what little he knew about the Chinese language from his consistent ordering at the restaurant down the street. There was a very slight variation in nasal tonation in Shu-shu's pronunciation which suggested that Shu-shu spoke more than one language. It was something he often heard in the voices of the bilingual people who came to read for him.

Dillon chuckled. "Of course he does. He wouldn't be able to operate the store if he didn't. But we made an agreement years ago that we would only speak Chinese to each other. It helped me to learn the language faster and it made sure his wife knew what we were talking about."

"Ah," Hunter nodded and turned to Shu-shu's voice. "You knew I wasn't a master. Why?" Hunter asked, thrusting his chin in the direction of where he thought Shu-shu's wife was cooking.

"She has waited many years. It was time," Shu-shu answered. Hunter heard the affection in his voice. But he also sounded weary and old, almost beaten. But now Hunter understood his logic.

Shu-shu was a practical man. He saw the opportunity in

Hunter's presence and took it with the hope that it would yield the results he sought. It made Hunter wonder if some of that same pragmatism had rubbed off on Dillon through the years. He was certainly more level-headed than Hunter would've assumed, considering everything he'd been through.

The smell of cooking food quickly began to fill the room and Dillon asked Shu-shu about who was minding the store and how things were with the business. He kept translating for Hunter as they switched back to Chinese so he wouldn't be left out of the conversation.

Food started hitting the table on large plates. Hunter was served before it was passed on to Dillon and Shu-shu. "This is awesome," Hunter said and listened as Dillon translated. Shu-shu's wife beamed again and Dillon passed on the nonverbal compliment.

Shu-shu began talking in earnest. Hunter noticed the din of cooking noises diminish as Shu-shu's wife turned her attention to the conversation between Hunter and Shu-shu. He knew something had changed, but he wasn't sure what. Shu-shu's wife interrupted a few times with more than a hint of irritation and disbelief, but Hunter didn't know what was said. Shu-shu seemed to close her arguments down rather quickly, but, once again, it appeared to be an argument which they had hashed through before.

Dillon was participating in the conversation but no longer translating. His articulation said he was more than surprised at what Shu-shu was saying, the sharp intake of his breath said he was stunned.

Rather than interrupt, Hunter continued eating. He liked the curious enthusiasm he heard building in Dillon's voice. Over the last few weeks, Dillon had been filled with despair, but this conversation was infused with the eloquence of hope.

"Shu-shu wants me to go into business with him," Dillon said after a few minutes of further dialog. "He said it would've been Bao's place. But now that he's gone…"

"Doesn't he have a daughter?" Hunter asked.

"That's what they're arguing about," he said of Shu-shu and his wife. "She's in college in New York and Shu-shu says she doesn't have any interest."

"Do they want you to take over the store?" Hunter asked.

"No, I don't think so. He hasn't given me specifics. I think he wants me to help him expand into something different. His original plan was to do import/export. He says with my grasp of the language I could do well."

Hunter tilted his head. "International sales kind of thing?"

Dillon laughed, a hidden excitement in his voice. "Yeah, can you believe that?"

Hunter stuffed more rice in his mouth. "Completely." Well, not completely, but he wasn't about to tell Dillon that. Maybe at some time in the future he'd sit down with Shu-shu and tell him how much he admired his quick-witted savvy. Not only had Shu-shu gotten his wife the answer she sought, but he'd handed it to her wrapped in a blanket of guilt concerning the man who had brought the 'master' to her doorstep. No wonder Dillon had thrived under his tutelage.

Shu-shu started talking again and went on for several minutes without Dillon's translation. It almost seemed as if he were admonishing Dillon for something.

"I don't understand," Dillon said to Shu-shu in English. "Why?"

Dillon went into a contemplative silence after Shu-shu answered his question.

"What did he say?" Hunter asked.

"He said life doesn't require my understanding or my permission to unfold. It does so on its own accord, whether I like it or not. He also said he thought I would've figured that out by now," Dillon replied.

"Have you?" Hunter asked.

"No," Dillon answered, still taking in Shu-shu words.

Hunter nodded, ate some more, and nodded again, lost in his own thoughts as he listened to them discuss Shu-shu's ideas. He understood. Dillon's question didn't just encompass Shu-shu's decision about the business plans. It went all the way back to the moment Shu-shu picked him up off the pavement behind the store. Maybe even before that.

Chapter 18

Dillon's house phone rang and they both froze. The ringtone said it was the security desk and their immediate fear was that Abigail had returned. Who else would be visiting unannounced? Hunter's chest tightened. He heard small measured breaths suddenly coming from Dillon as he tried to control his reaction for a potential second bout with his mother.

"Hang on a sec," Dillon said as he went to the phone. "Yes?" he answered. "Here? Send him up."

He put the phone down and came back to Hunter with obvious relief in his voice. "Roland's here. He's downstairs at the security desk."

"Roland? Your...the guy you worked for?"

Dillon glanced at him with an amused smirk. "My pimp? Is that what you're trying not to say?"

"Yeah, sorry."

"No need to be sorry," Dillon said. "That's what he was. I can't understand why he's here, though. He's never visited. You're the only visitor I've ever had. Well, you were until my mother showed up."

"Maybe he wants you back too," Hunter said. He'd meant it as a joke, but once the words were out of his mouth, the humor vanished. What if Roland really did want him back?

Dillon laughed. "No, Roland's not like that."

The knock came a few minutes later. Hunter heard Dillon open the door and listened as they exchanged greetings. He stood as Dillon invited Roland in and waited for them to approach.

Roland's grip was powerful and knuckle-scarred. Hunter determined he was a fighter of some sorts; a boxer maybe. Whatever he did in his time outside the agency, his hands were large and rough. He didn't have the grip of a martial artist, of that Hunter was sure. But there was fluidity in Roland's motion even if his actions were all solid and bulky. Interesting, Hunter thought.

"So you're the one who stole Dillon," Roland said as they shook. His voice was heavy but articulate. Definitely a boxer, Hunter concluded.

"And he has a grip," Roland commented as they released their hands.

"Nice to meet you," Hunter said and meant it. Roland felt personable, not the lurking street-baggage he'd assumed Roland would be. He wore an odd cologne too, something deep and broad across the nose, but mellow in strength. It favored his comfortable and assured grace.

"What are you doing here?" Dillon asked as he came and stood beside Hunter.

"Well, if you'd check your damned messages you'd remember the Christmas party is coming up and I wanted to invite you personally, both of you."

"I didn't think I was invited," Dillon admitted.

"Boy, your family. You'll always be family, and now Hunter

is a part of it. We'd like you there."

There was a silence and Hunter knew that they were both looking at him for a response. Was he Dillon's keeper already? "Sounds interesting," he offered.

"It's always a good time," Roland said, "very laid back, but a lot of fun. I'd love to have you both."

He was excruciatingly charming. Hunter was aware that it was probably the same voice he used for his best clients. "Sure," Hunter answered. "If Dillon wants to go, I'll tag along."

"Great," Roland said, rubbing his hands together.

Hunter heard fabric rustle and then felt the corner of a thick wad of paper against his hand. "Your tickets," Roland said as Hunter took them from him.

"Great," Dillon echoed.

Hunter thought Dillon sounded a little strained and slightly less than thrilled about the idea, but he said nothing. They offered their pleasantries and shook again as Roland blamed pressing business for his necessary departure.

"We don't have to go," Dillon said as soon as he closed the door and turned back to Hunter. "I'll just tell him I didn't feel up to it."

"Why does that sound familiar?" Hunter asked.

"I'm serious," Dillon said.

"Me too. He'll know right off that I didn't want to be there with your old clients," Hunter answered. His lips pursed in irritation at his own inability to keep his mouth from blurting out exactly what was on his mind. "Sorry, I didn't mean it like that."

"They're nice people, Hunter. These aren't street trolls. They were excited when I told them why I was leaving."

"What did you tell them?" Hunter asked.

"That I met someone and I wanted to give him all of me," Dillon answered as he took Hunter's hands in his. "Besides, it might be kind of cool to bring you down there and show you off."

Hunter smiled. "Yeah right. Doesn't he have this at his house or something? Why tickets?" he asked as he handed the envelope to Dillon.

"This is a big, private party with several hundred guests. Every year Roland rents out a venue downtown and hires a private security firm. The club will be closed to the public and only open to ticket holders. Everything is paid for, drinks, tips, everything. All we have to do is show up and have fun."

"I thought the service was very upper echelon, very discreet," Hunter said.

"Hence the private security," Dillon answered. "Roland will be introducing some of his new boys, so...discretion kind of takes a back seat when there's new meat on the market. You've got to understand, this isn't what you think. It's like a big, private, gay country club with benefits. You have to have the money to even be considered for membership. Then you need an invite from a member in good standing. Once Roland clears you, the other members will vote on whether or not you're in."

"All that for a piece of ass?"

Dillon laughed. "But only the best ass."

"Second best, I've got you now."

"Shh, don't tell them," he advised as Hunter pulled him into his arms and kissed him.

"Will they have music?" Hunter asked.

"Sure, it will be fully staffed. They'll have a DJ, food, all that stuff."

Hunter groaned internally but kept a smile plastered on his face. He knew he'd hate it, but he'd go for Dillon. His first and only attempt at trying out the club scene in Atlanta had been a disaster and he didn't hold any illusions that this would be much different. Private sex club or not, the only hope he had was that Dillon would be at his side. It might make the experience more enjoyable than the last time he'd been out on the town.

***

Dillon was snatched from Hunter's arm just a few minutes after they entered. Roland greeted people at the front door with a small entourage and as soon as they moved away from it, Dillon was whisked away, leaving Hunter standing somewhere near the entryway completely lost.

His temper rose instantly. He almost turned around and walked out, but he heard Dillon yell to him above the blast of the music and the people milling around.

"I'll be right there," Dillon called. But his voice was moving away.

Hunter waited for a minute, then two, but no Dillon. Instead, he was left standing in the middle of the room like a simpleton. His hand clenched and then unclenched around his cane. The warm welcome they'd met at the door now gone, he thought it likely that everyone was gawking at him as an oddity and wondering why he was there. And yet not one of these weak fucks had the courtesy to ask if he needed assistance; one of the few times in his life that he actually did.

"Fuck," he said under his breath. He pushed down his anger. He'd do this for Dillon and not act like a raging, pissed-off queen. But Dillon would hear about this.

"Where is the bar?" he said aloud, hoping someone was close or courteous enough to answer. No such luck.

The level of noise was completely disorienting, and his hearing, which he used to move around and get his bearings, was almost entirely shut down because of it. He stood motionless and tried to listen for the sounds of the bar above the noise. There was ice clinking into glasses, liquor bottles being pulled and put into place, beer bottles being opened, and maybe the sound of a cash register.

He blew out a long, frustrated breath and then moved to his left when he heard someone slam a beer cooler closed. It had to be the bar, and with everything free, the staff was probably running around like maniacs.

He bumped into a few people as he moved. He apologized and tried very hard to not show how upset he was. "Excuse me," he said as he bumped into another person. He kept the arc of his cane short and right in front of him, tapping people on their feet when they didn't move out of the way. One started to snicker when he turned to Hunter and his anger went into overdrive in an instant. "Can you point me to the fucking bar?" he demanded as his body swelled. He so wanted to drop this guy.

The snickering stopped instantly. "Right over there," the man answered before he shuffled off in the opposite direction.

Where the fuck is 'over there'? Hunter shook his head and continued on the same route, keeping his mental reference on the door he and Dillon had entered. The sound of beer bottles and clinking glasses grew and he followed the noise. When his cane struck the bottom of a bar stool, he sighed with relief. Now he had to figure out if there was someone sitting in it? He reached out with his hand and hit a shoulder. He felt the person jump slightly and turn at his touch.

"Sorry, is there an empty stool?" he asked.

"Over there," was the dismissive reply as the man turned away again.

His jaw clenched. Upper echelon my ass, he thought. The place was probably filled with wannabe A-listers whose only claim was the money their family willed down to them. They couldn't find anyone to tolerate their fake bullshit so they had to buy a piece of ass instead. And they didn't have manners worth shit. He moved down a few stools and ran his finger across the backs until he found one which started to spin when he put a light pressure on it.

Empty. He climbed up and allowed himself to relax a little.

Now all he had to do was figure out where the bartender was and get his attention. He needed a fucking drink before he seriously blew his cool. And Dillon, yeah. Where the fuck was he? With a fucking client, while he was stumbling around here looking like an idiot?

"What can I get for you?" a voice suddenly asked as a bartender appeared.

"Just a beer," Hunter answered.

He heard a bottle pop a minute later and assumed it was placed in front of him. Somewhere. Was there a glass? He hadn't heard one put down, but then a coaster would muffle the sound against the throbbing background noise.

"Enjoy," the bartender said, his voice already turned away and moving off to someone else.

"Yeah, thanks," Hunter muttered as his frustration abated. Thus far, the only thing right about this night was that everything was paid for. Otherwise, he would've been dicking around with the bartender trying to figure out how much the drinks were and what bills he got back in change. He hated this shit.

He sat for a few minutes and as he did so he became more infuriated. Dillon still wasn't around and he was sitting alone in a place whose layout he didn't know. He couldn't even take a piss because he had no idea where the bathroom was. If he climbed off his stool, he might spend the rest of the night scraping along the walls just trying to guess where everything was. You'd think that since Dillon had acted as Travis' guide, he would've known not to abandon Hunter in such an unfamiliar place. He tightened his grip on his cane and ground his teeth at the thoughtlessness. "So much for a fun night out."

"Another?"

Ah, the bartender. At least he wasn't completely ignored. "Yes, keep them coming. Where's the pisser?" Hunter asked. No answer. Was he talking to air? Had the bartender moved away so quickly? He heard another bottle put down in front of him a minute later and asked again before the man ran off.

"There's a couple of them," the bartender answered as his voice trailed off. "The closest one is behind you."

"Well, that's helpful," Hunter said quietly, under his breath. He sat for a few more minutes nursing his beer and then had another when the bartender magically reappeared again. He couldn't fault the guy. The place was loud and hopping and maybe that was why he was feeling increasingly resentful for allowing Dillon to drag him to a party like this. Of course, maybe it was the amount of beer he was drinking. Usually, two was his limit. But the fact that he was sitting on a bar stool in a club and was completely isolated from everything and everyone around him was only adding to his growing ire and he was sucking them down.

What the fuck am I doing here? Had they purposely invited him to make him look like a goddamned dependent jackass? Was that the reason Roland had personally delivered the invitation? And where the fuck was Dillon?

"Hey, sorry," Dillon said a little breathlessly as he came up behind Hunter and put his hand on his shoulder.

"Where the fuck were you?" Hunter demanded as he jerked his shoulder away.

Dillon was quiet for a moment, apparently shocked at Hunter's anger. "They pulled me out on the dance floor. I had to slip away. I'm sorry."

"The dance floor," Hunter repeated. He was irate in a heartbeat and chugged down the rest of his beer. "Do you think you could be bothered to tell me where the bathroom is before they drag you off again?"

"Come on, Hunter. I didn't do it on purpose."

"Bathroom," Hunter snarled.

"Would you like me to guide you?" Dillon asked.

"No," Hunter snapped. "Just tell me where the fucking thing is."

Dillon turned the bar stool slightly and pointed Hunter in the right direction. "Straight ahead about twenty-five paces. There's a small hallway which runs parallel to this room. Turn right and it's the second door on the left. Before you get to the hallway, there are three tables on your left and two on your right and about 50 people in between. Are you sure you don't want me to guide you?"

Hunter swiveled his head to him. "I've been getting around on my own for decades," he said with some heat in his voice. "I think I can find the bathroom without your help."

"Hunter..." Dillon said as Hunter took his first step.

Let just one of these bitches say the wrong thing, Hunter thought as he got to his feet. He came across his first human obstacle and said excuse me once before he rapped the stupid fuck on the shin with his cane. He heard the guy yelp and turn to him, but the man said nothing. Maybe he'd get the clue when Hunter came back out. Two or three more shin raps and a path seemed to open for him. Only one high-pitched, twink-sounding, young voice got shin-rapped after that and he started to say something sarcastic but then quickly fell silent.

Dillon, Hunter thought. He was probably right behind him staring these fuckheads down and daring them to open their mouth. He couldn't verify it because of all the ceaseless noise and the goddamn cologne these idiots splashed on. Bereft of both auditory and olfactic input, he was almost clueless as to what was going on around him and it pissed him off even more. He hated these fucking places. They wouldn't be so bad if they weren't filled with pretentious, perfection-seeking assholes, but they were. And anyone perceived as inferior was an object of jokes and derision.

He found the hallway and turned right, but Dillon hadn't said if there was a line or not. Fuck it, even if there was, he was going to the front and let anyone say different. He'd stomp the shit out of them and then call Margie for bail money in the morning. And when he was done pissing, he was going straight home. Fuck this shit.

The bathroom was just another reason he didn't do clubs. Once he opened the door, he'd have to figure out where the toilets and urinals were without putting his hands on every disgusting, cum-covered surface. Acoustics did nothing because they bounced so much, but if he were lucky then someone would be flushing and he'd have an idea of the layout.

The bathroom was silent and empty when he went in, there had been no line. He shook his head. It had to have been a first in the fucking history of gay clubs and just his luck. Maybe it was because it was so early yet. But it still stunk like every other club bathroom, a mixture of piss, stale beer, cum, and a lingering, chemical meth-flavored odor of sweat from all the drugs these morons dumped in their bodies. Dillon claimed Roland's boys didn't do drugs, but he honestly didn't believe it.

The door opened behind him and he stepped to the side. If he let the person go ahead of him, the noise he made would help him figure out where everything was. One thing was for sure, he wasn't touching anything in this room. He'd piss in the middle of the floor before he did that.

"Three urinals and two stalls on your right, and five sinks on your left," Dillon said. "I'm sorry, Hunter. They pulled me away."

"Save it," he told Dillon.

He moved to his right, swept his cane in a wider arc until he hit the wall and then raised it until he found one of the urinals. He unzipped and let go, his thoughts still hard and angry. He hadn't wanted to come to this party because he knew how this would go, and it had, just like he'd feared. Dillon's old clients had stuck their claws into him the moment they stepped into the club and dragged him off, leaving Hunter standing alone and fumbling around the place like a fucking idiot.

Dillon came up and wrapped his arms around him from

behind as his piss slowed to a dribble. "Get your hands off me," Hunter seethed.

"Hunter…"

"I said get your hands off me," Hunter growled again.

Instead of pulling away, Dillon pulled Hunter back against his chest and tightened his grip. "I'm sorry. I didn't mean for that to happen. I don't want you to be mad at me. Please," he begged.

Hunter reached up and grabbed the handle on top of the urinal to steady himself as Dillon pulled him off-balance. Already he was touching one of these goddamn disgusting surfaces. He pushed his anger down before he really lost his shit. He didn't want to hurt Dillon. He understood that Dillon hadn't planned it, but he should've foreseen it. Dillon could just as easily have told his friends to wait a minute and parked Hunter on a bar stool instead of allowing him to make a complete ass of himself. Or, he could've invited him along.

"I'm sorry," Dillon whispered again, pressing his lips into the back of Hunter's ear as he spoke.

Hunter blew out an angry flare of breath through his nostrils. Were they about to have their first argument? No. It was a thoughtless, careless mistake, but he didn't want to make a public spectacle of it. Maybe that was his mother's influence. "Can we go now?" he asked.

"We just got here."

"Dillon, this place isn't for me. I'd like to go home. This was a mistake."

"Okay," Dillon agreed, "but not just yet. There's still

something we have to do."

Hunter pulled in a breath and let it out slowly. He didn't want to be angry and he didn't want to make a scene, but he wanted out of this fucking club now. "What?" he demanded.

"This." Dillon started nibbling on his ear and snaked his hand down to grab Hunter's flaccid cock.

In spite of his anger, Hunter's body responded immediately. He felt himself swelling in Dillon's palm, the anger turning into a tempered lust as Dillon kissed the curve of his ear and nibbled down his neck. He was still pissed, but...God, he couldn't help but react when Dillon touched him.

"Someone will come in," Hunter muttered as Dillon gripped him tighter and took longer strokes on his growing cock.

"What if they do?" Dillon challenged him. "Every homo in this place has been lusting for you since we walked in the door. You turned every single head and it wasn't because of your cane."

"Then why the fuck didn't they help?" Hunter snapped.

Dillon chuckled, a low, sensuous laugh that was as alluring as it was indulged. "Don't you know how intimidated gay men are when they see someone like you, Hunter? You're fucking hot, and this is a private party so nobody knows who you are or how much power you have. These bitches wouldn't dare approach you. And you looked so pissed...so...mmm, angry and hot."

"You are so full of shit," Hunter moaned as Dillon continued to stroke him and nibble on his ear. His anger was almost gone. He couldn't help it. Dillon knew just what buttons to push. The spot behind his ear, the firm grasp on his cock, Dillon's small whispers, and the growing, hot bulge he felt against his ass.

"Roland could've booked you a dozen times over," Dillon continued with a husky voice. "They want to be dominated by you, Hunter. They want you to make them feel what you feel. Wouldn't you like that?" Dillon whispered as Hunter relaxed and tilted his head back against Dillon's shoulder. "You should've heard what they were saying about you on the dance floor."

Dillon curled his free hand around Hunter's neck and drew him back further as he worked his mouth into the crook of Hunter's neck. He lipped his Adam's apple and dragged a hot tongue back up to his ear. "All of them groveling for your cock, worshipping you...Can't you feel the power of it?" Dillon tempted him.

Hunter groaned. "Yes." His voice was hoarse with the lust of such a fantasy; his mind filled with the mingling of touches and smells which would come as they knelt around him. He could feel the different textures of their skin, smell their desire pushing out a menagerie of odors as each one's lust filled his nostrils...and their hands... Their hands would be a mixture of coarseness and refined softness roaming over his body; touching him, worshipping him.

He could feel the pressure on his larynx as Dillon pulled him back further, the movement accentuating the stroking of Dillon's opposite hand; the hand working his cock. He wanted that fantasy... He shivered as Dillon slowed and teased the very tip of his cockhead with his thumb.

"Should I open the door and let them watch?" Dillon asked.

"Should we make them want it? Make them beg? Can't you feel them at your feet already?" Dillon enticed him in a rough whisper. "Shall we make them worship you?"

Yes. Yes, he wanted it. He knew it and he knew Dillon knew it too. He'd make all these fucking bitches know the power of a blind man; know his power. They thought they were superior in this environment, thought they were above him with their glances and sideways looks and little snickers about his cane and his fumbling. Dillon was full of shit with his story, but he loved the crude thoughts that suddenly popped into his head about fucking in this filthy public place.

He moaned. It was just like his first fantasy of Dillon fucking him in a dirty hotel room. He turned his head and met Dillon's lips. His mouth was open, yearning as they kissed. The heat of Dillon's cock against his ass excited him and couldn't decide what he wanted more, to fuck or be fucked.

He and Dillon were a power here; dark gods come to walk among the little fuck boys and old men who wanted what they had: their youth, their vigor, and their muscled physiques. Maybe Dillon also told them he was a black belt when they were on the dance floor. He laughed at the thought. It would only add to the mystique — a queer, blind, ninja who would fuck you raw. He grinned. He rather liked the idea.

He let go of Dillon's lips and faced forward again, tilting his head to the side as Dillon nibble down toward his collar-bone. He felt Dillon's lips move against his neck and moaned. It left him completely breathless.

"Do you see now?" Dillon asked.

Hunter nodded slowly as Dillon continued to stroke. Yes, he saw. The sightlings were the odd ones out. They saw his relationship with Dillon and they were filled with envy. The hard bodies he and Dillon had, their small touches as they flitted against each other, the hot lust which sat so big and bold between them even at a distance. It was all a vast sign of the deeper feelings they had for each other. He suddenly didn't just want to fuck, he wanted to rut and scream and be the goddamned beast these bitches only wished they were.

Slick, Hunter thought, very fucking slick. Dillon wanted to put on a show and now here he was convincing himself of the same thing. This party wasn't just a meat market for Roland's new boys. Dillon wanted to show his old clients the finest cut available in the house and then deny them the ability to possess it. Hunter didn't know if he should be angry or flattered.

But maybe it was revenge that motivated Dillon. He considered the thought for a minute. Maybe this was a big fuck you to these people for all the years he'd had to service them to survive.

Fuck it. Dillon wanted a show? Hunter was going to help him give one, and he couldn't lie to himself. The expectation was already making him delirious with a raw animalistic carnality.

"Just us," Hunter whispered.

He felt Dillon smile against his neck and slow his strokes as he reached to unbuckle Hunter's belt.

"What if someone comes in?"

"Fuck them," Dillon snarled. Hunter could hear his lust with the direct and simple confirmation of his suspicion. This was revenge for Dillon, and the insatiable need for it was already gaining power as the thought of forbidden, public sex filled them both.

"No one touches you but me," Hunter instructed.

"Never," Dillon assured him, "Never." He finished fumbling with Hunter's pants and slid them to the floor with his boxers as he dropped to his knees.

Hunter moaned when he felt Dillon's hot tongue slide across the cheeks of his ass. He turned Hunter slowly; dragging his tongue and lips across Hunter's hip before he had him facing forward. He lapped at Hunter's pubes, blew on his cock once and rubbed his lips up and down its length before he swallowed it whole.

Dillon's mouth was hot and Hunter grabbed the urinals on either side to hold himself up as his legs buckled. The man knew how to give some head.

Dillon licked the crown with short jabs of his tongue, sucked off the pre-cum, and then crammed the shaft down his gullet so he could massage the entire length with the muscles of his throat. He bobbed on Hunter's cock, surging down to the root, rolling Hunter's nuts in his hand, and then pulled back to lick and tease the head by slapping it between his lips.

"Jesus Christ!" Hunter groaned and blew a breath out between clenched teeth. He threw his head back as Dillon slammed his throat down the length of his cock and began to swallow like he was riding it with his ass.

He could feel the drool from Dillon's mouth falling against the hair on his legs, the soft touch of his lips sliding over every rigid vein.

Hunter growled. "I want to fuck you." It echoed in the bathroom and came back at him like a snarl.

Dillon rose to his feet and took Hunter's hands. He led him over to the sinks with his pants shuffling around his ankles and his cock hard against the dress shirt he wore.

"Lube?" Hunter asked.

"Wait," Dillon said.

Dillon's clothing shifted as he moved away and then Hunter heard the mechanical shuffle of a dispensing machine as Dillon dropped bills into the slot and pulled the handle.

"Got it," he told Hunter.

He dropped to his knees again, ripped open the package and began stroking Hunter's cock, lubing it as he did. When he stood, he dropped his own pants and turned around, bumping his ass against Hunter as he fell forward over the counter.

Hunter reached around him and felt along the counter, his cock rubbing along the crack of Dillon's hot ass. "Can this hold you?" he asked.

"I think so."

Hunter grabbed him by the hair and jerked him back up. He turned Dillon so they were chest to chest. "Take your pants off, completely off."

Hunter took a step back to give him room and Dillon

complied without a word of protest.

"Now get on the counter and raise your legs," Hunter instructed him. He heard Dillon gasp in surprise when Hunter gave him a small shove on the shoulders.

Dillon wanted a show. He was going to get one.

Hunter took a leg in each arm and lifted. He slid into Dillon slowly, expanding Dillon's sphincter around his cockhead and allowing the lube to spread before he started pounding. He heard Dillon moan as his ass filled.

Hunter wasn't light or gentle with his touch. He could smell the hot, scented musk of Dillon's arousal; feel the heat from his erection. He inhaled the scent and let it roll across his tongue before he punched his cock in.

"Yes. Oh, God, yes," Dillon gasped. He grabbed the faucets on the sinks on each side as Hunter began to fuck him in earnest.

Hunter moved in a brutal, savage rhythm. He pushed Dillon's legs higher and higher until his pubic hairs were pressed tight to Dillon's nuts and Dillon was folded up on himself. He hooked Dillon's knees over his shoulders and impaled Dillon as he groaned.

"Oh yes," Dillon cried in a breathless whimper. "Yes."

Hunter fucked him hard but not fast. He slammed his cock in then pressed it deep, his ass cheeks tightening as he tried to drive his whole body inside Dillon's sizzling hole. His hips moved in a savage rhythm, the hard muscles of his legs rushing Dillon's ass, needing its hot warmth before retreating again into the cool stink of the bathroom.

He plunged in and dove forward, forcing Dillon's legs down sharp against each side of his head. He licked at Dillon's chin, swiping his tongue across the salty, lust-filled sweat that was forming on him. Fuck he tasted good.

Dillon sought his tongue, but he withheld it and continued to sample his damp fervor. The lust bubbled up in Dillon's throat and fell out in one long trembling breath. Hunter rammed his cock in deep and hard and hot as Dillon whined under the mastery of his torment.

The door opened suddenly and Hunter jerked his head in its direction, listening intently over the volume of music which flooded in.

There was a gasp and then, "Oh, excuse me."

The twink with the attitude, Hunter recognized the voice instantly. He was probably standing there watching them, his eyes wide and his young cock growing in the tight pants he undoubtedly wore.

"Stay." It wasn't a request. It was a command, one the boy followed instantly. Hunter heard the door close and he nodded. This was the perfect audience.

Hunter turned back to Dillon and tightened his grip. He picked up his speed and hammered his cock into Dillon's hot ass knowing he was being watched; knowing the twink would soon be wishing he was in Dillon's place.

There was a light whisper of noise as the twink moved tentatively across the tile. Hunter smirked. Even his steps were delicate he was so lithe. He was undoubtedly cute, maybe even beautiful, but not Hunter's favored body type.

Hunter heard the boy unzip his pants and begin stroking himself as he watched them. It made his cock harder as he pressed into Dillon with a renewed yearning. He wouldn't give the boy relief, but he wouldn't stop him from pleasuring himself either.

In a moment, the boy's hand was on his ass, a cautious, appreciative caress which asked for permission to do more. Hunter reached back, turned the boy's wrist, and brought him to his knees in one swift move. The kid gasped before he even realized that Hunter had locked his wrist. He hadn't stopped fucking Dillon.

"No touching," he instructed the boy and quickly let go.

The boy was at eye level with Hunter's cock now. Hunter felt his hot boy-breath pulse on his thigh as he fucked Dillon. He listened closely as the boy drew in the musk of their lust with a deep inhale. He wanted in on this action and it made Hunter laugh inside.

The music pounded in from the dance floor and thumped against the walls. Hunter matched its rhythm in hard, deep thrusts to accentuate the beat of the music.

Dillon was going crazy, thrashing and bucking his hips back against Hunter's invasion. His hands clawed Hunter's torso, reached for him, and then fell back to the faucets he gripped to keep him in place against Hunter's assault. He finally grabbed two fists full of Hunter's shirt and dragged Hunter down to his face. "You want to fuck him? You want to fuck his tight twink ass?"

Hunter shook his head no and heard the boy whimper beside

him. "Yes, please. Please."

His voice was light and young, the barely audible whisper of someone looking for a master to please. But Hunter wasn't the master for this boy. He wasn't a master and didn't want to be mastered. He wanted an equal, he wanted Dillon. He stood back up and continued stabbing his cock as far as he could get it into Dillon.

Dillon clawed his way upright when Hunter stood and thrust his ass down the length of Hunter's shaft. He sat vertical on the edge of the counter and made Hunter bend his knees as he took Dillon's weight. He rode Hunter's cock, pushing his weight down against Hunter's upward thrusts and then flexed his muscular arms against the counter to push himself back up again. He wrapped his arms around Hunter's neck, threw his full weight down on Hunter's length and put his lips to Hunter's ear.

"Finish in his mouth," Dillon offered in a harsh whisper. "Make this twink bitch understand." He let go and fell back against the mirror, curling his legs back and exposing his hole once again. He gulped in a breath and groaned as Hunter leaned deep into his ass.

Hunter picked up his pace and the bathroom was filled with the sound of his body slapping against the skin of Dillon's ass. He felt Dillon's muscles tightening and his nuts began to climb as his orgasm crawled into his shaft. Dillon's sphincter spasmed around him and he knew neither of them would last much longer.

"Come closer," he instructed the boy. He put his hand out until he found the back of the boy's head and pulled it next to the small space which separated him and Dillon. He threw his head back as his orgasm climbed and he continued to fill Dillon's furious need.

Dillon convulsed beneath him, the muscles in his neck standing out with a long silent moan as his orgasm mounted. Hunter could hear the boy panting and stroking beside him; his long, thin cock matching his years and the timbre of his voice.

Dillon's ass clenched around his cock one last time and Dillon howled as his own cum spurted hard and hot on his stomach. The boy groaned instantly and Hunter felt him lose his load hot and wet against his leg.

It was all too much; the aroma of hot cum, the boy rubbing his cockhead and panting against his leg. He pulled out of Dillon, grabbed the boy by the back of the head, and slammed his cock down his throat.

"Fuck...oh, FUCK!" He held the boy in place as every muscle in his body expanded, pumped, and pushed his cum out in long, thick spurts.

The boy squirmed under the pressure of his hands, choking on the sheer volume of cum. Hunter pulled back and let the kid breath momentarily and then slammed into him again, finishing himself as the boy gagged.

When he pulled out completely, the boy went to work, lapping Hunter's cock clean and sucking everything he could get from it. He rushed forward on his knees and rose up to lap Dillon's cum from his abdomen. Hunter staggered to the counter beside Dillon and put his hand down to lean on it as he caught his breath.

"Fuck," he gasped.

The boy was licking and slurping, running his tongue over every inch of Dillon's abdomen he could get to. When he finished, he shuffled to Hunter's side and sat back on his haunches. He leaned into Hunter's leg with his soft cheek and sighed. Hunter reached down and stroked the boy's hair. So very soft. He was just a young pup in the making and he didn't even realize it yet.

"Go on now," he said gently. He'd meant the boy no harm out at the bar earlier. He'd been frustrated and embarrassed and felt like a fool.

The boy nodded under his hand and rose, running his fingers lightly across both of their bodies before he stood, straightened himself, and then left without a word.

Dillon stood and grabbed Hunter into an embrace, driving his tongue into Hunter's mouth with the hot, devoted passion the boy was looking for.

Hunter smiled and pushed him back after their kiss. "We may want to pull up our pants before we get something else started." His cock was deflating and getting cold under the hard chill of the bathroom.

"I could go again."

Hunter chuckled and kissed him quickly. "Let's take it home."

"Okay," Dillon replied, planting a quick kiss on his lips before they began adjusting their clothes.

Hunter let Dillon look him over to make sure he was

presentable. He hated being dressed formally, but such was the attire. They both had a few wet spots here and there, but Dillon assured him they were unlikely to be noticed in the dim lights of the club.

Hunter listened to the music pounding on the bathroom door, the thump of it pulsing up through his feet. "This has to be the most unused bathroom in the history of gay clubs," he said, noting they were still alone.

Dillon laughed. "I've got someone on the door."

"You what?" Hunter smiled and shook his head. "How did the kid get in then?"

"I don't know. Nobody was supposed to get passed Lonnie."

"Lonnie?"

"Bouncer at the door when we came in," Dillon explained.

"Deep baritone voice?" Hunter asked.

"That's him. I gave him a twenty to guard the bathroom for a few minutes."

"So you planned this?" Hunter asked as he moved to the sound of Dillon's voice and reached for one of his hands. He took it and intertwined their fingers, bringing them to his mouth as he kissed each one.

"I figured we were either going to be fighting or fucking. I was hoping for the later, but I didn't want anyone interrupting either way. I'm sorry, Hunter. I didn't mean for it to happen. You weren't supposed to be left alone. I literally couldn't get to you."

Hunter reached up and caressed Dillon's cheek. He still

thought there was some planning involved in this, but he'd let Dillon have that. "Slick."

He felt Dillon smile and shrug under his touch. "Now you'll be able to remember this place with something other than a bad memory. And, maybe we can come back again," Dillon offered.

"If you don't leave my side."

"Right, won't happen again. Promise," Dillon added as he leaned forward and kissed Hunter.

"How old was the twink?" Hunter asked. He could still feel his softness, the down on his skin, the complete lack of any stubble on his face. He was so smooth it could've been a baby under his hand.

"Nineteen, twenty, not sure really. He's one of Roland's new boys. I haven't met him before. I think his name is Cory or something."

"Cute?" Hunter asked.

"He's beautiful," Dillon admitted, "if you like boy-toys. And as we now know, eager to please. Did you like him?"

"He was very...soft. Even his voice sounded vulnerable."

Dillon chuckled. "That's probably why Roland picked him up."

Hunter tried to picture the boy for a moment. He seemed like such a fragile, svelte, little thing trembling under his hand. Delicate, that was the word which came to his mind first. He shrugged it off, not his type but definitely interesting. "Can we go home now?" he asked Dillon.

"Well," Dillon said dragging it out. "Cory is probably breathless out there with all the details of our little escapade. Maybe you want to wait around a bit and let it get fully around the club?"

Hunter smiled. Dillon really did want to show him off. "Slick, like I said. Are you going to leave my side?"

"No, but once that kid is done, I may be spending the night in jail when I start decking some of my old clients for hitting on you."

Hunter laughed. "I thought you said it wasn't that type of crowd."

Dillon smirked. "It's not, but sex like that…you never know."

Hunter considered it for a moment. "All right. Now that they know who the boss is," Hunter teased, "we can hang for a few."

They made the rounds and ended up staying another three hours. Hunter listened for the slight vocal inflections above the blare of the music and knew Dillon had spoken the truth. A few of them had appreciation and desire in their voice. By the end of the night, he had no doubt that everyone in the club would know what had happened. But maybe Dillon had planned it. Perhaps the twink had been sent in for just that reason. So they'd know Dillon had found an equitable mate and that he was no weak, simpering, little blind man clinging to Dillon for affection.

He squeezed Dillon's hand once as he led them to the door and smiled to himself. Even if Dillon didn't do it on purpose, it was still one of the hottest fucks he'd ever had.

Chapter 19

Christmas Eve

Snow had begun to fall and Dillon put the phone down. He and Ah-tam had spoken about her parents and his increasing involvement in their business. It turned out she didn't want anything to do with it. She'd been more than happy to hear that Shu-shu had offered him a partnership because she had no desire to leave New York. It seemed Ah-tam's mother had her own ideas. She was going to find Ah-tam a husband worthy of the family business and make sure she came home and had grandchildren. Ah-tam had other plans.

"Goddam it," Hunter grumbled from the other room.

Dillon smirked. It was a wicked little grin that curled up one corner of his mouth. Ah-tam had just given him permission to take her father's offer and the business in any direction he saw fit. Her trust lifted his spirits.

He now had goals. And he had Hunter in his life. But there was one more thing he wanted. He'd planned on waiting, but while he was talking to Ah-tam he realized that he'd been waiting his whole life. Waiting and worrying and losing out on things. Something about the snow had changed his mind. He went to the bedroom.

"Ready?" Dillon asked from the doorway as he watched Hunter fumble with his tie.

"If I can get this fucking thing put on properly."

"Are you sure about this?" Dillon asked.

Hunter stopped and turned to the sound of his voice, a vexed look on his face. "It's the symphony, Dillon."

"That's not what I'm talking about," Dillon said as he walked over knotted Hunter's tie for him.

"I'm sure," Hunter answered. He'd officially given up his apartment and would be out by the beginning of the New Year. Dillon had already arranged to have movers empty the apartment the day after Christmas.

"You realize that means tonight will be the first official night in our place," Dillon remarked as he pulled their heads together. "It's snowing outside," he added, kissing Hunter.

Hunter sighed into his kiss, pushing his lips firmly against Dillon's. "I love the snow," he muttered as Dillon pulled away. He put his jacket on. "Are you ready for my mother's house tomorrow?"

"I'm ready for anything now," Dillon answered.

"Travis will be there."

"I don't care. How are things with him and your mom, anyway?"

Hunter shook his head. He had no idea. "I am not asking my mom about her sex life. Sorry. It's bad enough I walked in on them."

"What?"

Hunter closed his mouth. "I never said that."

Dillon started laughing. "Oh, you're going spill this."

"No way."

"But I can picture them getting it on rather than getting all pissed off when I see Travis tomorrow," Dillon teased him as he walked across the room. He reached up on the top shelf of the closet, grabbed something, and then closed the door. They were running late, but with the snow he wouldn't have been surprised to learn that half the city was running behind schedule.

"I am not talking about my mom's sex life," Hunter reiterated.

"Hunter?"

Hunter turned to his voice. The sudden change in Dillon's tone was matched only by the abrupt stillness that came after it.

"I keep thinking I need to wait," Dillon said as he walked back to Hunter. "That it's not the right time or the right circumstances. I'm tired of thinking like that. I'm sick of living in the past and being cautious. I found what I want."

Hunter put his hands on his hips. "What the fuck are you talking about?"

Dillon came to him and got down on one knee. He took Hunter's hand. He knew Hunter could probably feel him shaking, but it didn't matter. He wasn't about to wait anymore. "You've pulled me kicking and screaming into the center of a circle I never knew existed. I refuse to give that up. Now, or ever," he added as he put a small box in Hunter's hand.

Hunter gasped.

"You can say no because you're worried that it's too soon or that things are going too fast. But I'm going to keep asking over and over again until you say yes. Will you say yes? Will you marry me?"

Hunter opened his mouth, but no words came out.

Dillon took one of the matching rings from the box and took Hunter's index finger in hand. "I had these made special. The design is raised instead of carved in. Can you feel it?"

Hunter ran his fingertip over the outside of the ring. He nodded as a tear formed in the corner of his eye.

"Can you tell me what it is?" Dillon asked quietly.

Hunter's voice choked. "Two people…"

"Two men," Dillon corrected.

"Two men," Hunter said, "pulling each other into the center of a circle."

Dillon watched Hunter's single tear slip and start sliding down his cheek. "Would you step into the circle with me?"

Hunter nodded, a small sound escaping him. "Yes."

Dillon stood, thumbed his tear away and kissed Hunter deeply. He pulled back and smiled as he looked at him. Hunter was still in shock and tongue-tied. "Did I tell you it's snowing outside?"

Hunter nodded. His hand was shaking slightly as he continued to rub the inscription on the ring.

"Snow is kind of weird," Dillon continued. "It's so slow. It drifts a little here and there and it doesn't make much noise," he said as he looked at Hunter. "I think I want to skip the symphony." He untied Hunter's tie and slipped it from around his neck. "I would rather we stay in and see if you can match its rhythm. What do you think?"

Hunter smiled. He didn't nod. He took a step forward and put the second ring on Dillon's finger and led him to the bed.

THE END

Learn about Brandon's other books on his website at

BrandonShire.com

~

If you liked this book please don't forget to leave a review and share it with your friends on Facebook, Goodreads, Twitter, and wherever you purchased it.

~

About the Author

Award-winning writer BRANDON SHIRE is a distinct voice in contemporary LGBT fiction. Mr. Shire was chosen as a Top Read in 2011, Best in LGBTQ Fiction for 2011 & 2012 and garnered several Honorable Mentions, as well as a Rainbow Award for Best Gay Contemporary Fiction. He resides in the South.

You can find out more at BrandonShire.com.

Other books by Brandon Shire

The Love of Wicked Men

Sid Rivers and Jack Brown are two sides of the same coin. One is a lawyer with his own firm and dreams of money and power; the other is a criminal with a lengthy record and a quest for vengeance. When they meet, sparks fly. But was their meeting an accident? Or was it planned by the billionaires who want to control their destiny?

The Love of Wicked Men is an erotic journey into the underbelly of the legal profession, the corporate culture of profit-at-any-cost, and the secret world of industrial espionage.

Cold – Gay Romance Series

Prison is a brutal, heartless, and demeaning environment. No one knows this better than a man sentenced to life in prison for murder. Lem Porter has given up, but when he finally meets someone who captures his heart, he soon realizes that there is more to life than just the walls which surround him.

AWARD-WINNING LITERARY LGBT FICTION:

Summer Symphony

A bisexual father loses his daughter to stillbirth and has no mechanism to cope until one man comes along and shows him the power of music, and the strength of a father's love.

Listening to Dust

When love blossoms unexpectedly and is then ripped away, a world shatters and a man with it. (RAINBOW AWARD WINNER)

The Value of Rain

Chronicle's one young man's journey into the world of 'reparative therapy' and reveals the destructive nature of families, secrets, and revenge. (BEST IN LGBTQ FICTION 2011).

CPSIA information can be obtained
at www.ICGtesting.com
Printed in the USA
BVHW042114081220
595228BV00031B/810

9 781480 289857